German Lessons

Frank Hannaford, a young Australian from a sheltered
Catholic background, is searching for a deeper version
of himself in 1930s Germany. At the university and in an
organisation of young Catholic men he finds friendship and
a new confidence in his own resources. A German identity
begins to form, surprising and delighting him. But he also
struggles with the unexpected possibilities of love, and
with political events and commitments he does not fully
understand. The Nazis come to power, previously strong
opposition from the Catholic Church evaporates, and Frank is
left floundering, at odds both with himself and with the young
woman whose friendship he most values. A *Bildungsroman* set
in a time of social and political upheaval.

for Mariko — and in memory of Toshio

A Novel

German Lessons

KIERAN DONAGHUE

PALAVER 2019

Acknowledgements

While imbued with history, as documented in the Chronology, this story is essentially a work of fiction, of imagined characters and situations and of possible responses to real events. Anyone who knew my father may recognise aspects of him in Frank's father, but the other fictional characters are modelled at most superficially on people I have known or read about.

I would like to extend my heartfelt thanks to Ngaire Donaghue, Paul Komesaroff, Sally Gardner, Barry Donaghue and Mariko Nakamura for their encouragement and textual advice. I would also like to thank the ACT Writers Centre for arranging appraisals of early drafts, and the appraisers for their constructive criticisms. Without the help received from these sources the book's shortcomings would be much more extensive than they currently are. The responsibility for the final product is of course mine alone.

Kieran Donaghue

For additional information, bulk or educational purchases, and other resources, please contact Ethica Projects, Pty. Ltd c/o Paul Komesaroff: paul.komesaroff@monash.edu
First Palaver Edition published July 2019
Cover design and layout: Ian Robertson

www.palaver.com
Palaver is an imprint of Ethica Projects, Pty Ltd.
10 Barnato Grove Armadale Victoria 3143 Australia

Contents

I
The Table : October 1932

Saturday 1 October 1932

There were polite questions about Frank's journey, then an awkward silence. Father Klein sat back and surveyed his young visitor. He spoke slowly. 'It was a great sorrow to me when your father left the seminary. But I am sure it has been for the best. Of course you must think so.'

'Yes, I suppose, if my father had become a priest, I wouldn't exist. Which is not an easy thought to understand.' Frank took a moment. 'Well, to understand it is easy enough, as a matter of logic, but to feel its full meaning, that is much more difficult. And...unsettling.'

'I see you have a philosophical bent. That reminds me of your father.' The priest laughed briefly to himself. 'Yes, we called your father "the philosopher". Thomas Aquinas was his leading light, the great synthesiser of ancient wisdom and Christian doctrine. I must admit, that sort of thing was not my strength. It passed over me like water over stones. And left me just as rough as before.' Father Klein's hands pointed to his considerable bulk, or perhaps to the signs of unkemptness in his clothing. 'But John – he so loved to argue the point. Every point. At any time.'

Frank was not sure he had a philosophical cast of mind, but he was quite happy to talk about his father. And he was particularly pleased that the priest's Bavarian accent, although unfamiliar in its rhythms and cadences, was proving easy enough to understand.

'My father studied philosophy when he returned to Australia. But he always saw it as the servant of his religion. He said the philosophers at the university discovered this and did not like it. For them philosophy was the queen, not a handmaiden. So my father decided to give it up.'

'But he seems to have done very well in his chosen calling.'

'He sells insurance. But things are very difficult at home now. With the unemployment.'

Father Klein let Frank's words slide away. He continued to reminisce. 'Your father was a very good friend to me when we were in Rome, I hope he has told you. I'm afraid my Italian was poor. I think I have no talent for languages. Many people here say that I cannot even speak German.' Another small laugh. 'But your father spoke excellent Italian and also some German. That was a godsend to me. And he was most generous with his time. A very honest and sincere man. That is how I think of John. Do you also speak Italian?'

'My father always wanted me to learn, but the school I attended didn't offer it. So I just learned German. And Latin. Six years of Latin.'

'You have two sisters, I think.'

'Yes, both younger than me.'

'Are they healthy and well, your sisters? And your mother? I think she should be heartily congratulated for marrying such a fine man.'

Frank thought that if there were any congratulations to be handed out the recipient should be his father. He was sure his dad would agree. But it was neither the time nor the place to say this.

'Thank you, they are all keeping well.'

The conversation ebbed and, as Frank cast around for something to say, the door opened and a large woman with grey hair tied back tightly came into the room. She was carrying a tray with coffee things and cake. She set the tray down heavily on the priest's desk.

'How would the young man like his coffee, Father?'

'You must ask him yourself, Frau Wolters. Herr Hannaford will be staying with us for some time, as we discussed, so you will need to know how he takes his coffee and such things.' Father Klein added, largely to himself: 'What we call coffee, at any rate.'

'Would you like milk in your coffee, Herr Hannaford? There is a little sugar in the bowl. And help yourself to a piece of cake. I could not find any vanilla, but I do my best with what God sees fit to give us Germans.'

The woman turned back to the priest. 'Father, I've prepared something cold for the evening meal and for tomorrow. There should be enough for you and your guest. But you and I will need to talk again about the household budget, the extra expenses, about how we will manage, with the collections falling off.'

Father Klein responded that prices were also falling, or at least were not rising, but Frau Wolters dismissed this with a tightening of her mouth.

Despite the reference to budgets and prices Frank enjoyed this exchange. When the priest had been speaking to him he had sensed significant effort being expended to accommodate his presumed lack of ear for the German language, at least for the priest's version of it. He had a similar feeling from the few words the housekeeper had addressed to him. But the two native speakers had no need to worry about such things. Their speech was natural and unencumbered and he thought it beautiful, even if he did not catch every last word. He found himself practising the phrasing and intonation in his head, testing them on his tongue, before leaving them to be savoured again later.

When Frau Wolters had left the room Father Klein confided to Frank: 'She has not had an easy life. Husband long gone, son with the reds. She has a great love for her country and feels a deep humiliation, like so many here, about what has happened. But she is very loyal to me. And there is a warmth there, you will see.'

'I understand Father. I feel I am coming from a very sheltered place.'

There was a brief discussion of when Frank's board would fall due, when and where he would take his meals, laundry arrangements, other practicalities. The priest then prepared to stand, but changed his mind and settled back in his chair. 'You know, it meant a great deal to me when I received the letter from your father after the World War. I had not long moved here from my previous parish and I was finding it difficult to settle in. And I think all Germans felt very much cut off from the rest of the world at that time. We were the vanquished, even though no foreign forces had ever set foot on our soil. And it seemed to us that we were being blamed, unfairly blamed, for all the destruction and the suffering. To receive the letter from your father, written in the German language, with its words of friendship and concern, and after so many years. This was a wonderful thing. A bridge to something better. I still read that letter from time to time.'

As he sat there, enjoying the warmth of the atmosphere, Frank realised that his father had told him very little about Father Klein. Even when it had been agreed that he would stay at Father Klein's presbytery during his year at university in the Rhineland, a year on which he was staking immense but vague hopes, his father had not told him much about the priest. But this reticence was perhaps not surprising. It was more than thirty years since his father had seen Werner Klein.

'I remember I was embarrassed when I included in my reply to your father details about my clothing and shoe sizes and asked if it might be possible for him or other sympathetic Australian Catholics to send me something, second hand things. I even asked if he could send some vestments for the Mass. And some months later I received three very large boxes full of clothing and tinned food, even some chocolate. And shortly after that another letter, this time with more information about the family. The material things were of course most welcome. But the friendship and care, these were the most important things. And John's pride and happiness in his family, this gave me deep satisfaction. I could feel our Lord taking great joy in this family. And here you are, John's son, sitting with me in my presbytery. It seems like a wheel has come full circle.'

Frank felt a surge of pride in his father and love for him. He resolved to do everything possible to be a credit to his father in Father Klein's eyes.

The room that was to be Frank's was located at the rear of the presbytery. It was small but neat and tidy, with minimal furnishings. There was a crucifix on one wall and a worn rug on the floor, a bedside table that rocked as Frank laid a hand on it and a stolid looking wardrobe that seemed to preside over everything.

He sat on the bed and thought that, rather than finding everything strange and difficult, his arrival had been a form of homecoming with much that was familiar. He had foreseen so many difficulties in his first meeting with Father Klein, anticipated so many missteps, that its actual course now seemed to have been laughably easy.

Frank looked around the room again. There was a desk and a chair but he realised they were much too small. He imagined Father Klein rushing to the parish school and grabbing what was nearest at hand, a last minute thought. Something would have to be done, but it could wait. The priest had mentioned a tram stop, to the right at the front gate of the presbytery and a little way along on the left hand side. He set off to explore the town.

Thursday 6 October 1932

The 'mensa', all the students called it, the table. Frank liked that. He liked the feeling of unity and purpose and solidity it conveyed. But in fact there were rows and rows of tables, and as he looked around he could see that they were filled with young men, a smattering of older ones, occasional young women, everyone talking and gesticulating and laughing as they ate and drank. He was sitting alone, but he felt in good company.

He took a piece of paper from his pocket and unfolded it on the battle-scarred table beside his plate. He was eating noodles, trying to keep the sauce from spilling onto his clothes, every now and then stopping to glance at the note. Copies had been everywhere, stuck on notice boards and tucked under salt shakers and anything else that would hold them in place. They contained an invitation to all foreign students to attend a get-together at the foreign students' office.

It's tomorrow, Frank realised. There might be someone there with whom he could compare notes.

He had spent nearly three years at university at home in Australia and had enjoyed it immensely. His parents had been so proud. His dad had said that 'uni' was doing him the world of good, it was 'bringing him out of himself'. But this tone changed when Frank brought up the possibility of studying in Germany. His mother looked to her husband to say something to quash the idea, but Frank quickly pointed out that his father had gone to Italy when he was only nineteen. His dad's response was that he had been sent to Italy, he had not just gone there, and he had not been alone, he had been immersed in a brotherhood of care and support. And anyway they would not be able to afford it, not the way things were heading.

The topic lay dormant. Then, some months later, his father matter-of-factly delivered the news that Werner Klein, a fellow student at the seminary in Rome all those years ago, was offering Frank a spare room in his presbytery.

Frank had been at the beach with Ellie and Margie. The ocean was a ten minute walk from their house and it was there that he and his sisters spent nearly every morning in the hot January weather. When they got home they went around to the back of the house as usual to wash the sand off their feet. Frank turned the garden tap on full-throttle and, a ritualistic practice, pressed his finger against its mouth to generate a sharp stream of water. Margie was the first target but she blithely skipped out of harm's way. When Ellie's turn came she just turned her back and hissed: 'Oh do stop it Frank.' His father opened the back door and stood, demanding. 'Frank, stop the yahoo behaviour and come inside. I've got something to tell you.'

Frank turned off the hose and examined his feet. He had walked barefoot from the beach over the low sand dunes and the stretch of scratchy bitumen until he had got to the couch grass near the front of their place.

His mother thought that couch was ugly, with its blunt, stubby leaves, but she had to accept that the salty sea air was too harsh for more refined grasses. Frank liked the couch, its sponginess encouraging against his bare feet. He had a pair of old sand-shoes with him but could not be bothered putting them on. In fact he hardly ever wore them, and by the end of the summer the soles of his feet would be as hard as bits of old leather. Every now and then he would use one of the sand-shoes to give Margie a smack on her backside or the back of her legs, but he never really made much contact. She would fling her hands behind her as if shooing away a fly and then duck and weave, enjoying the dance. Ellie was now too old for this game. And she had never been a willing player.

'Well Frank, I've mentioned Father Klein to you. After we spoke I wrote and told him you had got it into your head you wanted to study in Germany. I asked if he had any contacts who might be able to help.'

Frank's father had been holding a letter in his right hand as he spoke. He put it on the table.

'Well, Father Klein writes that he has a spare bedroom in his presbytery and he is open to giving you the use of it. Of course we would have to cover the cost of your food and other things, but the amount he mentions is not beyond the realm of possibility.'

'Dad, that's extremely kind of Father Klein. But where does he live? Which uni would I be attending?'

'He lives in an old town in the Rhineland. It's called Siebenkirchen.' Frank's father picked up the letter to confirm the name. 'Yes, Siebenkirchen, seven churches.'

Frank's mother stood silently during this conversation. Then she went to Frank and put her arms around him and clung to him, the top of her head nestled under his chin. His father extended his hand and Frank shook it, still pressed against his mother.

'Well, young man, this looks like it might come to something. You need to think carefully whether it's what you really want. You would know no one there. There would be temptations. You would be thrown back on your own resources.'

Frank felt a sudden loneliness in the pit of his stomach. 'Yes, I will Dad, of course I will.'

Back in his room the gathering heat and the lassitude induced by the morning's sun and sea overcame Frank and he quickly fell asleep. He woke after a short time and sat hunched over, playing with his imagination. He tried to visualise Father Klein's presbytery but could not get past a pale version of the presbytery of his own local parish. He tried to picture Father Klein, to hear his voice, but his father had given him little to go on. And he wondered what the temptations were that his father had envisaged.

He woke very early the next morning to a silent house. He ate some toast, grabbed his swimming things and headed to the beach. The long stretch of sand was deserted, although he could see a pair of surfers lying on their boards, gently rising and falling on the swell as they waited for a wave. He stripped to his togs and waded in, bracing for and then accepting the first shock of cold, turning and dipping his knees to allow the water to wash over his torso, then his shoulders and his head. He lay floating on his back and started to stroke slowly with his arms and gently kick his legs, feeling his body respond to the reassuring lift of the water. When he was well beyond the breaking waves he turned over and began to swim, a slow crawl. He let his mind empty of all but the occasional thought that he should head back in. 'Soon,' he said to himself.

Finally he began to tire. He allowed the tiredness to seep fully through him then turned and let himself float again, arms and legs barely moving. He raised his head and looked towards the shore.

The beach still looked deserted, but he was so far out that he could not be sure. He felt a fleeting brush of fear, but then lay his head back and let the water lift him up. The fear ebbed and was gone and in its place was something like exhilaration.

—

A young woman came and stood across the table from him. She gave him a quick look and asked: 'Ist hier noch frei?' He swallowed awkwardly and mumbled 'Ja'. The woman's tray rattled onto the table as she sat down.

Frank's first impression was of a high forehead, dark eyes, an active mouth. He hoped she would not speak again. He focused hard on his eating but then thought this might be too obvious and felt himself begin to blush.

'I saw you at Mass,' the girl said. 'Father Klein introduced you to my parents. My mother is the organist. And she takes the choir.'

'Oh yes.' Frank remembered a tall, slightly stooped man of his father's age and a still-attractive woman who had been friendly enough but who had said little and seemed distracted.

'My name is Anja.'

Frank said his name, making sure to pronounce the vowel the German way. Not 'thank you Frank' but 'danke Frank', a little word-play he had made up and sometimes shared with himself. They shook hands.

'I'm not sure how to tell you. You'll think it's rude. But you have a very unusual face.'

There was a half-smile in the girl's eyes, a challenge. 'And you're very tall,' she added, 'even when you're sitting.'

Frank kept his mouth closed as he chewed a mouthful of spaghetti, buying time.

'I suppose you mean my nose.' His hand went to his face and adjusted an imaginary pair of glasses. At times he had thought that glasses with heavy frames might help disguise the size and shape of his nose, the unmistakable sharp bend about a quarter of the way down its long path. But his eyesight was perfect and feigning the need for glasses was not something he had ever seriously contemplated. He knew they would not really have helped.

'It suits you. You shouldn't want to change it.'

'Whether I'd like to or not...'

There was a pause.

'You're foreign, aren't you? You're English?'

'In a distant, far-flung sort of way.'

Anja did not say anything, but her look told Frank she had no idea what he meant. Before he could explain Anja was speaking again.

'You think I'm forward. I don't mean to be. My father says I'm brash. My mother says I'm inquisitive. I prefer my mother's opinion.'

A pair of young men approached the table. There was an exchange of greetings with Anja but little breaking of stride as they headed towards the rear of the refectory. Frank took the opportunity to observe his companion's face. He noticed that the skin around her mouth and eyes seemed to have a life of its own and he felt an urge to smooth away the excessive movement.

'Theo and Carl,' Anja said, answering Frank's unspoken question. He waited, but there was no elaboration. Instead Anja searched in her worn leather satchel, produced a packet of cigarettes and offered one to Frank.

While they were smoking Frank became aware of a commotion behind him. He turned and saw a group of youths in dark, uniform-like shirts standing at a table where two young men were quietly eating. One of the group slammed his fist on the table and his companions raised their voices to the point of shouting. The two at the table tried to carry on eating, but this seemed only to spur on their tormentors. There were calls from several parts of the mensa for the agitators to stop, and a pair of burly students stood up and looked like they were ready to back up their words with actions. With a few parting shouts and gesticulations the aggressors made their way past Frank and Anja's table and out of the mensa.

'What was that about?' Frank asked. 'Who were they?'

Anja's answer was a look of disgust that unsettled Frank even more than the incident itself.

'My brother Lukas was with them,' Anja said eventually.

Before Frank could formulate a response Anja was on her feet, holding out a hand for a parting handshake. 'It was nice to meet you, Frank. Perhaps we'll see each other again.'

Then she was moving away, slim and angular. When she was out of sight Frank realized she had a limp.

Friday 7 October 1932

There were only a few people on the street when Frank got to the old building that housed the foreign students' office. A nondescript youth in the entrance hall immediately pointed to a room at the end of the corridor. The door was ajar. Frank knocked gently, waited, knocked again, then slowly pushed the door open and edged his way inside.

Three young men were standing together not far away, each holding a drink, appraising him as he entered. 'I'm looking for the foreign students' party,' Frank said. 'Have I come to the right place?'

'Well that was quite an entrance. Real polite I'd say. Wouldn't you say, Charles, Raymond? Real polite. What's your name, young man, where are you from?'

The only American accents Frank had ever heard were in the handful of talking films he had seen at home, but he suspected it was American-accented German he was hearing.

'I'm from Australia. My name is Frank Hannaford.'

The young man who had spoken first continued, this time in English. 'Well, Frank Hannaford, right pleased to meet you. I don't think we have anyone at this fine old university from Australia, so you're a first. Well done to you, sir. You want something to drink? I suggest you get yourself a beer. I seem to remember from somewhere that Australians like beer. By the way, I'm Bobby, this is Charles, and Raymond.'

There were handshakes all round. Then Frank, slipping into English like it were a favourite pullover, declared that he was very pleased to meet them all and they were the very first Americans he had ever spoken to, assuming they were Americans. They confirmed they were.

'That's quite an accent you got there, Frank,' Bobby commented. 'I would have picked you for one of our English cousins, but I'm not

18

real strong on accents. We got a few limeys here, you know. Maybe some will come by tonight. You can talk to them about cricket. I think you all play cricket, right? Sounds like the weirdest thing. Goes on for days. Maybe you can explain it to me some time.' Bobby patted Frank condescendingly on the shoulder. 'But not tonight.'

Bobby was about average height, solidly built, with sandy thinning hair. He was wearing a jacket and a bow-tie.

Frank was still casting about for a suitable reply when a shabbily dressed young man added himself to the circle. The immediate impression he gave was of rubber, probably due to his lips, which were thick and sinuous and took up a disproportionate part of his broad, brown face. And then there was the hair. Unkempt would have been a generous description. A dishevelled pageboy, with a sandwich in one hand and a bottle of beer in the other.

'Look what the cat's dragged in.' Bobby and the others seemed especially pleased to see the new arrival. There were handshakes, vigorous from the Americans, less so from the newcomer, while Frank stood on the periphery, torn between the thought that he should get something to drink and a desire not to miss any of this encounter. 'Jak, great to see you. Brown as a bean, lots of sun and sea back home. But no barbers, from the look of it.'

Bobby's German was good. Not the accent, that was not quite right, the American intonation too apparent, but the vocabulary was wide and the sentence-structure sound. And the idiomatic flourishes, they were perhaps a bit overdone, but impressive nonetheless.

As Frank made this assessment he resolved to catch up to and even surpass Bobby. He was confident in his ability. He had a good ear, his teachers had told him so many times, and he had never groaned at grammar like his classmates. He had always been happy to lose himself in the parsing of a sentence, burrowing down into the innards of the language, taking apart and reconstructing with a new understanding of the mechanics of meaning. All this would stand him in good stead.

Jak was saying, his mouth full of chewed sandwich: 'At home, what's there to do? So I came back.'

Bobby waited while Jak took a long swig of beer. Then he said: 'I was under the distinct impression that you were not on board with the impending change in political direction in this country. Or did I get that wrong?'

'Politics are shit everywhere.'

Bobby laughed. 'Not one to mince words, are you Jak? No indeed. A straight talker. We like that, don't we?' Bobby looked at his companions for confirmation.

'No girls?' Jak said, looking around. 'I thought you were getting girls.'

Bobby appeared unruffled by Jak's remarks. Adopting the tone of a teacher explaining a simple problem to a slow student, he asserted: 'Jak, you know we are working with limited resources. There just aren't many young ladies among us foreigners. And because they are so scarce, the ones who do exist are not inclined to come to gatherings such as this, because they feel – and, I have to say, who can blame them – that they are likely to be set upon by young men such as you and given no peace.'

Frank felt embarrassed at the direction of the conversation. He looked around the room at the groups of young men, none of whom he recognised.

'I won't stay here,' Jak said. 'I want to play table tennis.'

At this point Bobby's gaze fell on Frank. 'You should have spoken up. Jak, allow me to introduce a newcomer to our ranks. This is Frank, and Frank is from Australia. What do you say to that!'

Jak offered his hand. 'Jak, from Brittany.' He turned to the others. 'We have enough English speakers already.'

Frank bristled, but he said to Jak: 'I promise, whenever you're around I'll speak only German.'

'Too many English and Americans in their own little groups, I don't like that. I don't go running after French speakers the whole time.'

'Jak, please descend from your high horse,' Bobby lectured. 'Why would you run after French speakers? You dislike the French even more than you do us Yanks or the Brits, or even the Boche. You'd want to be chasing after Breton speakers. And I dare say there aren't many in this town.'

'I've found one. But he thinks he's French, so not much use.'

The Americans laughed and Frank joined in. He was warming to Jak.

Jak finished his beer, scrutinised the empty bottle and then wandered off. Bobby said to Frank, in English: 'A suitable name, Jak, don't you think? All that wayward hair. It's a wonder he can see where he's going.' Bobby seemed to enjoy Frank's look of incomprehension. 'Can mean a yak, at least the spelling.'

Frank knew a yak was an animal of some sort but he had no idea what it looked like. He started to sketch possibilities in his mind, using Jak as a template.

Jak returned with another bottle of beer, and another sandwich. Bobby made to put an arm around him but was shrugged off.

'After this bottle I'm leaving.'

Oblivious to Jak's remark, Frank said, a thought suddenly coming to him: 'Breton's a Celtic language, isn't it?'

'Bretons are Celts. Like the Cornish and the Welsh and the Scots.'

'And the Irish. My grandparents were Irish. One was Scottish, I think. Anyway, that's interesting, isn't it?'

'I don't think so. You play table tennis?'

Bobby said that Jak and Frank should go along and enjoy their Celtic heritage. He looked at Frank. 'I toyed with all that at one time, but now I've moved on.' He added, in an affected Irish accent: 'O'Donnell.'

Charles Smith pursed his lips. 'Jak, best be careful. Things have got a bit rough here over the summer. Plenty of fisticuffs, and worse.'

Jak shook his head and Bobby said to Frank, in a conspiratorial tone. 'Keep an eye on him. He invites trouble. No shortage of young louts around happy to oblige.'

Frank shook hands with the three Americans, then hurried to catch up to Jak.

—

'Where's your bike?'

Frank replied that he did not have a bike.

'Should have a bike.'

They set off together, Jak wheeling his bike, Frank despite his long stride needing to quicken his steps to keep up. The evening was warm and there was a faint smell of something rotten coming from the river. The light of day was showing no sign of abating.

'I live quite a way from the uni so I catch the tram.'

'Move into the old town. All the foreign students live there.'

'I couldn't afford to move. I live with a priest and pay only a small amount for room and board. I don't have much money.'

'You a theologian? Too many theologians at this uni.'

Frank explained how he came to be staying with Father Klein. He went into detail. The contrast to Jak's careless tossing out of words seemed to give his German increased fluency. He felt himself briefly in a position of strength.

'You should stay away from priests,' Jak responded. 'Where I come from they're like gods. Everywhere you turn, a priest. They smell.'

Frank said nothing. He thought he should defend Father Klein, priests in general, but he did not know what to say. The parish priests he had known had been unexceptional. His father and mother had respected them and he did too. That was it, as far as he was concerned. Except for the occasional sense of a mismatch between ordinary men and their extraordinary ability to intercede between God and man.

'Why come here anyway?' Jak asked. 'No decent "unis" in your country?'

'I could ask you the same question. Why are you here?'

The answer was swift and the sentence well constructed. 'This country is going to shit, and I want to have a front row seat.'

Frank responded with a nervous laugh.

'Not a joke. If you stay here very long you'll understand. Most serious thing in the world.'

Nothing more was said during the few remaining minutes it took them to arrive at their destination. Frank saw a large shop on the far side of the street with a handful of figures bent forward at the display windows, pausing, looking, hurrying after their companions. An occasional motor vehicle chugged past, asserting for a few moments ownership of the narrow thoroughfare. Jak propped his bike against the steps of an old building and they went inside. Frank had not been paying attention while they were walking and he had no idea where they were. What Jak had said about Germany had unsettled him, knocked him off balance.

Off to one side of the entrance hall Frank caught a glimpse of a smoke-filled room with desks and typewriters. Jak went straight past this room towards the rear of the building. There was a door on the right which he opened without knocking. Inside there was more smoke, but instead of desks with typewriters there was a billiard table and a table tennis table and a smattering of young men, some smoking, some drinking beer out of large greenish bottles. Two or

22

three lazily raised their hands in greeting as Jak and Frank came in.

A game of billiards was in progress but the table tennis table was quiet. Jak strode to a dilapidated book shelf at the far end of the room and rummaged around in an old cardboard box. He extracted two table tennis bats and a ball. The bats were in a condition befitting their storage place, the rubber surfaces worn and in one case the wood underneath exposed.

'Best you've got?' Jak asked no one in particular. He offered the scruffier of the bats to Frank and pointed towards the table.

Frank knew immediately he was out of his depth. He struggled to keep the ball in play as they warmed up, his long reach his only advantage. Jak humoured him for a short time only before he started to whip the ball inaccessibly around the table. When Jak suggested that they play a game Frank could see impending embarrassment, but he could not see a way out.

Jak was clinical and merciless, making no adjustments to accommodate the shortcomings of his opponent. On the rare occasions when he was not happy with a shot he shouted 'Merde!' and refocused his efforts.

'Show some mercy, Jak,' one of the beer drinkers called out. 'Don't be such a brute!'

The second game followed the same pattern as the first. Jak again made no allowance and the game was soon over. He said that was enough for tonight.

As Frank made to hand the bat to Jak a strongly-built man of average height appeared out of nowhere and intercepted it.

'Max.' A smile briefly illuminated Jak's face. He gestured to the table and readied himself to serve. A game was quickly underway.

The newcomer's movements were precise, his eye excellent and his demeanour relaxed. Jak by contrast was a picture of intense concentration, his rubbery features now taut, sweat on his neck, a hand constantly pushing his hair from his eyes. A number of the billiard players left their table and threw their support behind Max, but despite their encouragement he could not sustain his initial energy and Jak soon began to dominate. Eventually Max stepped back from the table and raised his hands in admission of defeat.

Jak threw down the bat. 'Let's go for a drink,' he said. 'Proper drink in a proper pub.' He was already heading for the door. Frank and Max shared a brief look of complicity before setting off after Jak.

Frank trailed behind. He got outside and could see Jak and Max in earnest conversation, something about keeping your eyes peeled. Then he realised how late it was.

'I'm sorry, I have to go. I think I've missed the last tram. I'll have to walk home.'

'Where do you live?' Max asked.

'In the country-side,' Jak answered on his behalf.

'Near Werderstraße,' Frank said nervously. 'But I'm not sure of the way.' He was looking around, wondering which direction he should head in.

'It's too far to walk,' Max said. 'You'd better stay with me, though it'll have to be on the floor.' Then turning to Jak: 'Sorry, not tonight for the pub.'

'Go by myself then.'

Frank offered his hand to Jak, who shook it without enthusiasm. Max and Jak nodded to each other and Jak got on his bike and rode off into the night.

'It's just his way,' Max said. 'You'll get used to it.'

Max started to wheel his bike and Frank fell into step beside him. He realised he had not introduced himself and began to explain where he was from and why he had come to Germany. To immerse himself in the language, to strike out on his own, to break the mould of his life. Max asked a few questions and Frank responded eagerly, searching for words that would demonstrate he was worth the effort Max was expending on his behalf. But gradually Max's interest abated and he seemed to withdraw into himself, his demeanour turning into a mild rebuff. They walked for several minutes in awkward silence. Then without any preamble Max announced that he was not sure now was the right time for what Frank had in mind.

They reached the market place, not far from the mensa, and Frank felt his sense of isolation dissolve in the familiarity of the cobblestones and the surrounding houses with their accentuated timber frames. He began to enjoy the walk, the rhythm of their footsteps and the soft rolling of the bike wheels, the stillness of the night, the dull wash of the street lights replacing the retreating daylight. But the peace was suddenly disturbed by a group of youths who were spilling out of a building on the other side of the square. There was a surge of loud talk and shrill laughter. Frank slowed to look but Max abruptly motioned to him to keep moving. It sounded like one of the group was addressing them out of the distance, taunting or threatening, the others urging him on. Frank hurried to catch up to Max. The voices receded, then swelled again, seemingly reluctant to release their grip. Finally they fell away, leaving Frank short of breath.

They turned into a narrow lane and Frank saw two women leaning against the side of a building, smoking cigarettes. One of them called out something. Frank was not sure if the words were directed at him and he quickly replayed them in his mind. As he did this the other woman approached and held her arms open. 'Hallo dearie. Like me to keep you warm?' Frank instinctively pushed at her, as if she were a large spider suddenly there on his bare skin. The woman spat out a curse and lurched back to her companion, who laughed roughly as she threw away her cigarette.

There were several more lanes to traverse and then several sets of stairs to climb before they reached Max's tiny room. A bed, a small desk and chair and a lopsided wardrobe took up almost all the available floor space. Max fetched a couple of thin blankets from the wardrobe. 'Spread these on the floor at the end of the bed. With your height, you might not be able to stretch out fully.'

'The bed I have at Father Klein's isn't long enough for me.'

'I know Father Klein.' Max was looking hard at Frank. 'My mother is his housekeeper.'

Frank struggled to take in this information. He was occupied with the sudden realisation that he should telephone Father Klein, to explain what had happened. He had seen a telephone box in the market square, and Max said he would go with him. 'But if we come across any brownshirts look straight ahead and keep walking.'

In the half light outside Frank thought he recognised one of the women who had accosted him, in conversation with a man. Then he heard a voice, loud and clear, from the other side of the lane. 'Changed your mind have you dearie?'

Frank felt suddenly emboldened. He stopped and called back. 'Vielleicht ein anderes Mal. Perhaps another time.' He felt Max's hand on his arm, steering him away.

Monday 10 October 1932

Anja sat down in the mensa opposite Frank. She smiled unconvincingly. 'I didn't see you at Mass yesterday.'

'I went to early Mass. It leaves more of the day for other things.'

Anja fidgeted with her bag and her cutlery. Then she blurted out that she did not like Father Klein, had never liked him. 'My parents are close to him, with the choir and everything. And my elder brother Michael, holier than thou. But I've always kept my distance.'

Frank wanted to speak up for the priest, but he waited to hear the charges that Anja would bring against him. Eventually Anja finished eating and pushed her tray aside.

'There were Nazis at Mass yesterday, full of false solemnity. Ernst Tüchnow and Arnie Wriedt and the rest. They were holding up a large photograph of Lukas, dressed in a brown shirt, flowers around the frame. They had no right to be there.'

'I'm so sorry about your brother.' Frank was aware of the inadequacy of the words, but could think of nothing better.

'They didn't come to the funeral, they were warned to stay away, but they were there yesterday, in their vile uniforms. And Father Klein did nothing.'

Anja sat still, her eyes seemingly focussed on a distant object. Then her animation returned. 'Papa went to challenge them. There was a scuffle and he fell and hit his head. But Father Klein said nothing.'

'He probably didn't see, Anja.'

'Everyone was looking.'

Frank could imagine the scene, heads turning surreptitiously, curiosity winning out over piety.

'But Michael stood up to them. He sent them packing.' Anja paused, then concluded: 'I think Father Klein is a Nazi.'

Friday 14 October 1932

They had arranged to meet at the door to the hall where the music evening was being held. Frank got there well before time and stood trying to look inconspicuous as people began to arrive, mostly in groups, talking quietly and being together. He was relieved when he saw Anja, but taken aback to see that there was someone with her. 'This is my sister Cordula,' Anja said to Frank as she came up to him.

The young woman with Anja smiled and gave Frank her hand. The hand felt slight, almost weightless. Frank registered the large brown eyes and full lips. All other details were submerged in an overwhelming impression of something quite lovely that left him not knowing where to look.

The room they entered was not a concert hall. There was no stage and it was not very large. There were rows of wooden chairs, enough for fifty or sixty people. The front rows were full and Anja led them to a row half way back. They moved to the centre, first Cordula, then Frank, then Anja.

Frank slipped his satchel under the chair and then went through a clumsy manoeuvre to get his jacket off, apologising to both sisters as he did so. Anja leaned across him and spoke to her sister. 'The bald man in the front row, near the end, he's the lecturer I told you about. He's not exactly handsome, is he?' Cordula shook her head, whether agreeing that the man was not handsome or rebuking Anja for her comment Frank could not tell.

He wondered where the musicians were. Not only was there no stage but there were no chairs with music stands and no piano. He turned his head and saw two young men enter the room, one carrying a gramophone, the other a pile of records. They set the apparatus up on a small table at the front of the room.

'It's a gramophone,' Frank said.

'Yes it's a gramophone,' Anja responded briskly.

'I was expecting musicians. I thought a small group, a piano.'

The bald man who had been the object of Anja's remarks went to the front of the room, raised his hand for quiet and then welcomed everyone to the evening, especially the students who were new to the German faculty, and of course any guests from outside. He hoped everyone would enjoy the music. There would be wine and cheese during the interval. He returned to his seat to unfocused applause.

One of the young men went to the gramophone and began to tinker with it. Frank heard hissing and crackling, then the first strains of a piano, then a man's voice, a tenor. The sound was soft and Frank had to strain to hear. But he recognised the melody; his mother played it sometimes on the piano at home. A voice behind him called for the volume to be turned up. One of the technicians scurried forward and made some adjustments.

Frank held himself stiffly between the two sisters, arms pressed into his sides, legs together. But despite this effort he felt a surge of enjoyment being where he was. The soft scent of newly washed skin and hair, coming from Anja or from her sister or from both he was not sure, relaxed him. And he could sense the shared listening and focusing and attending bringing them imperceptibly together.

When the record finished Frank felt a touch on his shoulder and a young voice asked politely if he could slide lower in his chair, the people behind him were not able to see. Anja turned and interjected that there was no need to see, you were supposed to listen. But Frank, now feeling himself ungainly, began to slide down. 'Don't Frank. You won't be comfortable. Stay where you are.' Anja had her hand firmly on his arm.

When the new record began Frank was distracted by the tension emanating from Anja and his mind lost contact with the music. His back started to ache and he felt trapped. He struggled to breathe. When the piece finished he got awkwardly to his feet and motioned to Anja. He worked himself with difficulty past the row of listeners until he reached the aisle, then tip-toed to the rear of the hall where there was a free seat. He looked to see whether his escape had attracted attention, but could see no heads turned in his direction.

At the interval Anja came and asked if he would like some wine and they went together to the refreshment table at the side of the room. Frank saw Bobby the American out of the corner of his eye but did not look in his direction and he sensed Bobby moving away.

28

'Your sister must think me rude.'

'Cordie never thinks ill of anyone.'

Frank glanced up from his sweet wine and caught sight of Anja's sister talking to a young man with a round face and a guitar case firmly grasped in one hand. Anja turned to follow Frank's gaze. 'That's Felix. He's in my brother's Vanguard group. He's in love with Cordie. But don't worry, she's not in love with him.' She added, in a quieter voice. 'They're all in love with Cordie, although they won't admit it. Especially to themselves.'

Skirting the subject of love, Frank asked Anja what a Vanguard group was.

'Earnest Catholic boys who think they can save their own souls and save Germany at the same time.'

Frank tried to catch another glimpse of the young Vanguard member, to see him in the light of what Anja had just said, but she continued to demand his attention.

'And who think their hearts are made for more than the love of a girl.'

All this sounded to Frank like something Anja had rehearsed and was glad of the opportunity to recite. But he was still intrigued.

In contrast to the first part of the program the music after the interval was dramatic and voluptuous, a rush from climax to climax, within the limits of the gramophone's capacity. It invited in Frank feelings of indulgence and excess and he found the invitation oppressive, a form of emotional bludgeoning. He tried to uncover a melody, something simple and obvious to hold on to, but was left with the thought that all the pleasing melodies may have been used up by the time these pieces were written. There must only be a finite number.

Then the bald man was on his feet again, thanking everyone for coming and giving special thanks to the technicians who had made everything run so smoothly, and to those who had organised the wine and cheese. There was a round of applause, then a pushing back of chairs and general movement and talk.

As he waited Frank saw Bobby O'Donnell leaving the room in discussion with a studious looking young man with oriental features. Neither appeared to notice him; they were engrossed in their conversation. Then Anja and Cordula appeared and Anja handed Frank his jacket and satchel and he responded with a sheepish look and a few words of thanks. As they made their way out of the building it occurred to Frank that, apart from a simple 'hello', he had not spoken to Anja's sister yet. He tried to compose a first sentence, but nothing suitable came to mind.

Anja's father was on the far side of the road, walking backwards and forwards beside a large dark car. He lifted his hand in a beckoning gesture when he saw his daughters, and Frank felt himself included in the gesture.

When everyone was settled in the car Anja said: 'Poor Frank. Someone in the row behind asked him to slide down because he couldn't see. What was there to see? There was just a gramophone. But Frank slunk off to the back of the room for the rest of the night. Frank, you should stand up for yourself.'

'Leave Frank in peace,' Herr Auer said.

'Of course, Papa, what's more important than peace?'

'Cordula, hold your sister's hand. That will calm her.'

'I *am* holding her hand, Papa.'

Cordula and Frank exchanged a smile.

Friedrich Auer drove with both hands firmly on the steering wheel, bending forward and peering at the road. He inquired cursorily about the music and Anja said it was very nice but he should concentrate on his driving. Nothing further was said until the car pulled up outside Father Klein's presbytery.

'I can't forgive him, Papa. From now on I'm going to Mass at St. Agnes's, to Father Schapp. I won't come back here.'

'Not now Anja,' her father and sister said almost in unison.

After this exchange the occupants of the car sat in silence, not moving. Then Herr Auer turned to Frank and said he hoped he would find what he had come to Germany for.

'Thank you, Herr Auer. I'm sure I will.'

Monday 17 October 1932

Anja was nowhere to be seen. There was a man at their usual table, slightly older than most of the other students and with what Frank took to be Chinese features, faintly familiar. With no better alternative he went in this direction. In response to his question whether the place was free he received a slight inclination of the head. He took off his coat and looked around. He thought he recognised the two young men who had greeted Anja that first time, but they were deep in conversation with a larger group and paid him no attention.

'It's busy in here today,' Frank said as he sat down.

The oriental man had a plate with tomato sauce and meat balls in front of him but was not eating. He was sitting up straight.

'This food is very bad. I will never get used to it. Often when I approach the mensa I think I will not be able to go in. The thought of the food affects my stomach. But there is little alternative. I have no cooking facilities where I live. Each day I read the menu at this mensa and also at the smaller mensa near the river and choose which is likely to be less bad. I try to eat without thinking about the food and without paying attention to the taste. Sometimes I succeed. Mostly I do not.'

Waves of noise were lapping around them, carried by a warm vapour rising from bodies and plates and coffee cups, but the quietly spoken words bobbed on the surface, precise and measured.

'I didn't realise there was another mensa.'

'In Königsallee. Many of our orientalists eat there. The atmosphere is more intimate. But that is not relevant to the quality of the food. And of course our social scientists up on the hill have their own mensa. But I have never eaten there. It is too far.'

Frank was ravenous. He had chosen sausages with gravy and mashed potatoes, and it looked and smelt inviting. But he held back out of solidarity.

31

'You were at the music evening,' his companion said.

'Yes, of course. You were with Bobby.' Frank remembered clearly now. But the American's surname escaped him. 'With the bow tie.'

'Tsu-to-mu,' the man said, extending his hand. 'But Stormy will do. They all call me that.'

Frank took the proffered hand but he forgot to introduce himself, unbalanced by the English word. 'Stormy?'

'My family name is Ueda. So I am Ueda Tsutomu, in the Japanese way. But Westerners put the given name first, so Tsutomu Ueda. Stormy Weather. The Americans find it amusing because I have a calm disposition, so they say. Do you understand?'

Frank nodded and Stormy Weather started to eat, palpably without relish. His nostrils tightened. Frank also ate, making an effort to moderate his enjoyment.

'The Japanese characters in my name suggest someone working diligently in the rice fields. But I have never worked in a rice field. Nor have my parents. They are educated people. My father is a school teacher, my mother's father was a writer. He prepared a Japanese-German dictionary. He was a very knowledgeable man.'

'What is your field of study?' Frank asked, pausing from his food. 'If you don't mind me asking.'

'I study philosophy.'

'My father studied philosophy when he was young, but he didn't keep it up. Sometimes I wonder whether I should have studied philosophy. What's it like?'

Frank remembered his brush with philosophy in the German course at university back home. They had been told at the beginning of third year that they would read some philosophical works in second term and he had looked forward to it. But when they were handed a typed copy of extracts from Nietzsche he had been taken aback by both the difficulty of the language, which swelled and crashed like an angry surf, and the confronting nature of the content.

The lecturer had encouraged his students with the comment that it was high time they engaged in some iconoclasm, and Frank, a timorous creature in his own eyes, had braced himself. In the event he had enjoyed the sharp thrill he had received from the invitation to philosophise with a hammer. But the argument that good and evil were obsolete had unsettled him. And the bragging and chest-beating that seemed to crop up at regular intervals had grated. Yet none of this had stopped him returning over and over to the texts. He wanted to understand every word, to master the exuberant language. And he wanted to develop his own views on the content before raising the subject at home. He would practise the arguments beforehand with several of his classmates, testing his thoughts before putting them into the field against his dad.

'You need to be more specific,' Stormy Weather said. 'What do you mean, what is it like?'

'Well, how is it different from theology, for example?'

Stormy put down his knife and fork and pushed his plate away. He seemed to be weighing up whether he should reply, and if so in which register. Finally he said: 'Theology is about a particular object, albeit an object of a special kind. Philosophy does not have an object like this. It is more about a way of thinking. I would say it is an attempt to understand the most basic concepts we use when we think about and interact with the world and with our own selves.'

'So philosophy is thinking about thought. Can you say that?'

'I do not think that quite captures what I am saying. We interact with the world and with our own selves in ways other than through thought. We feel things, for example. Philosophy is also about analysing what feelings are.'

'But feelings don't use concepts, do they? And you said philosophy was about concepts.'

Frank thought he had made a good point. He leaned forward and rested his elbows on the table and propped his chin on his hands. Then a shadow glanced across the table and Anja sat down abruptly, organised her things and began to eat.

Frank sat back. 'Hello Anja. This is Stormy.' He corrected himself. 'Tsu-to-mu. Tsutomu is from Japan.'

Anja put down her knife and fork and shook hands with Stormy. She said she might have seen him in the mensa before.

Frank offered, concentrating on his articulation: 'Stormy is a philosopher. I was asking him what the difference is between philosophy and theology.'

'I have no patience with the theologians,' Anja responded. 'They say God is beyond our understanding and then spend all their time trying to understand Him. Faith is a feeling and you can't reason about it. You either have it or you don't.'

Frank tried to read Stormy's reaction to Anja's gust of words, but he could not. It did not seem that his companion was going to respond, so he interjected: 'But sometimes our feelings let us down. We can't always trust them.'

Stormy stirred and said quietly but emphatically that it is our beliefs that let us down. 'But beliefs are really feelings,' he added.

Anja spoke with her mouth half full. 'More and more about less and less.'

'But don't you think these ideas are interesting and worth studying?' Frank pleaded.

He had not understood Stormy's last sentence. As far as he was concerned beliefs and feelings were very different, almost opposites, but he nevertheless felt called on to defend a long and venerable tradition of thought. Then he wondered whether he was usurping Stormy's role and started to feel out of place.

Without warning Stormy gathered his things together, stood up with his tray in one hand and a bulky briefcase in the other, said goodbye and left. Frank and Anja sat there, watching him glide away. Then Frank explained the origin and meaning of the name Stormy Weather, but if Anja understood the humour she gave no indication she appreciated it.

'Did you notice?' she asked. 'He hardly blinks. His eyes just stare.'

'I knew there was something.'

Frank felt protective of Stormy. He realised instinctively that Stormy's good opinion was something that would be hard to earn but worth the effort. He changed the subject. 'Do you really think faith in God is just a feeling?'

In place of an answer Anja picked up her satchel and fumbled around inside it, extracting a sheaf of papers and handing them to Frank. 'This is what they'll be talking about tomorrow night.'

Frank flipped though the pages. 'I don't think I can read all this before tomorrow.'

'You won't have to say anything. Michael does most of the talking.'

'I'm very grateful for the invitation,' Frank said. 'Please thank your brother for me.'

'Make sure you're waiting outside the presbytery. I don't want to see Father Klein.'

'Seven o'clock?'

Anja nodded. Then she said: 'Cordie's beautiful, isn't she?'

Frank tried not to react but he could feel himself redden. Anja placed her hand on his forearm. Then she abruptly withdrew her hand, collected her things and left.

II
The Vanguard : October – December 1932

Tuesday 18 October 1932

They were greeted by the sound of applause. Anja bowed, stood to one side and extended both hands, as if presenting Frank to an admiring audience. Frank felt the blood shoot to his face. He heard his father's voice. 'Stand up straight!'

When the noise died down he could hear Anja asking: 'Michael, where should Frank sit?'

Frank turned towards the person Anja was addressing. He was tall, a slender build, thick light-brown hair swept back from the forehead, thin serious face, frameless glasses perched high on the nose. For an instant Frank felt he was standing in front of an older and less jarring version of himself.

He glanced around the room. He saw Anja's father and her sister sitting on a sofa. There were two other chairs, high severe backs and faded upholstery. Anja's brother had been resting a knee on one of the chairs but was now standing fully upright.

The other chair was occupied by the round-faced young man from the music evening. He was hunched over a guitar, sounding gentle chords. The rest of the room was full of young men strewn about, sitting or reclining on the floor, some on cushions, others on folded blankets.

They have been singing, Frank realised, remembering the sounds that had helped to calm his nerves as he and Anja were climbing the stairs. And when they finished they were so full of the music and their own enthusiasm that they applauded themselves. He could feel traces of their eagerness still in the room and see it on their faces, a clear contrast to the dull colours of their clothing. He saw that the guitar player was stealing glances at Cordula. He has been playing for her, Frank thought.

'I think with your height you may need to sit on the sofa,' Michael Auer suggested.

Frank summoned his concentration, stepped carefully through the press of bodies and reached the sofa. Cordula moved a little closer to her father and Frank managed to turn and sit without mishap. The room remained quiet during this process, seemingly anxious lest something should go wrong.

'You know my father and my sister Cordula,' Michael continued. 'I won't introduce the others. There are too many of us. You'll get to know everyone else during the course of the evening.'

Frank expressed his thanks. The simple words felt heavy on his tongue as they blundered their way out.

'You are the first foreigner we have had at one of our meetings. So of course we are very interested in your impressions. Please be forthright.'

Frank said something non-committal in response to Michael, who turned his attention to the group. 'I hope everyone has brought their copy of the Holy Father's encyclical.'

A flurry of rustling followed as papers were produced from pockets and bags. Frank retrieved the copy Anja had given him.

'We finished the last time with a discussion of communism, why the Church is so opposed to this doctrine. I hope you all remember.'

A tentative voice asked Michael to summarise what the Holy Father said about the communists.

'You will remember there was an earlier encyclical on the subject of work. This was prepared by Pope Leo in 1891. At that time communism was receiving a lot of attention as a possible solution to the problems of modern society. Pope Leo was critical of communism because it sought the abolition of private property. But he was also critical of liberalism. He recognised that a free market was widening the gap between rich and poor. He wanted a middle way.'

Frank could feel the concentration in the room. He let himself relax into it.

'It is not just the rejection of private property that the Church finds fault with in communism. It is also the fact that the communists do not want to overcome class conflict. They want to sharpen and intensify this conflict until it erupts in violent revolution. This revolution the Church understandably rejects.'

A light, pleasant voice came from a corner of the room, a complement to Michael's intensity. 'Our Lord was a revolutionary. So the Church can't be against all revolutions.'

Concerned looks appeared on a few of the faces, amused looks on others. Frank wondered how Michael would respond, but it was Anja who spoke, looking directly at the interjector, challenging him.

'You know that the revolution Our Lord called for has to take place in our hearts. It has nothing to do with the revolution of the communists.'

The room went quiet. Michael, his breathing audible, asked if anyone else had questions. There was some awkward shuffling. Then a hand went up.

'Yes, August?'

'I like the part where the Holy Father says that above all else we should help the weak and the poor. That's right, isn't it, Michael? That's what our religion teaches.'

'Yes August, it is,' Michael said reassuringly.

'And our politicians? Let the poor and the weak go to the devil, and the Catholic Party in Berlin going along.'

'Jochen, you know our meetings are not the place for party politics. We should focus on what the Holy Father is telling us in his encyclical.'

'I'm sorry, Michael. I'm impatient, you know that.'

Frank had the impression that this last exchange, in one form or another, was a regular feature of these meetings.

Another voice intervened, heavier, more measured. Frank turned to find its source. He saw blond hair sharply parted at one side, a long face. 'The Holy Father is critical of liberal capitalism and of communism. So there is a vacuum. If the Church is not able to fill this vacuum with what is good, others will fill it with evil.'

—

Harald Halbach, the owner of the long face, was older than the others, all except Michael, but he had only recently joined the Vanguard. He had known for some time that groups of young Catholic men were forming across the country, crystallising out of the hiking associations that now seemed to be past their peak. They wanted to create a new form of Catholic consciousness, so Theo Lindner had said when encouraging Harald to join. Harald had not found Theo's explanation of this new Catholic consciousness very illuminating. He had given more weight to the words of Father Schapp, his parish priest, who had told him that Michael Auer's group needed members with experience of the world of work, to keep everyone's feet on the ground.

But still Harald had resisted. He had not joined the hiking groups, although he enjoyed the open air, and he had kept his distance from the Vanguard. Probably this was due to a feeling that, when it came down to it, the Church was on the side of the owners rather than the workers, and that the Catholic associations, even those of the young and of the workers themselves, unwittingly shared this bias.

It was Max Wolters who had confronted him. Max was a typesetter at the printing works where Harald was employed. Harald knew that Max came from a Catholic family and had lost his father in the World War, but they seldom talked about these shared things. Max always seemed preoccupied. So they remained colleagues, skirting the edges of a possible friendship.

Then one day Max had attached himself to Harald after work and they had walked together until they came to Harald's building in the workers' district.

Max had said that the only solution for Germany was a socialist one. Either an international and outward-looking socialism as the great pioneers envisaged, or so-called National Socialism and the road to perdition. He had to choose. 'Otherwise you'll just float on the tide, a piece of flotsam.'

While Harald was preparing a response Max had looked up and down Jakob Lane and said that the Nazis were planning to march through the workers' district the following Sunday and that some of them might stray this far. Such a provocation would necessitate a strong response; there would be violence and he should be careful.

Harald could not join the socialists or the communists. He was Catholic and they were godless and there was no reconciling the conflict, whatever Max might think. But he did not want to be a piece of flotsam. He doubted the Vanguard was the answer, but he saw no better alternative. And he wanted to get to know Michael Auer.

—

Harald's intervention was followed by a gap in the discussion. Then Jochen muttered something and Michael asked him to speak up.

'To fill the vacuum, a national community.'

Frank could feel Cordula's body stiffen beside him. Jochen went on, a burst of justification. 'Not all the Nazis want a new war. They want the government to pay for buildings and roads and give jobs to the unemployed.'

The room hushed and everyone looked at Michael.

'These things are well and good, Jochen, perhaps even necessary. But beneath the surface? Worship of violence, purity of race and nation before belief in God. There can be no accommodation with this movement.' Michael waited, but there was no response. 'We have been through all this before,' he said abruptly, closing the subject.

In the lull that followed Friedrich Auer pushed himself to his feet and made his way out of the room, gesturing to the others that they should stay where they were. He gripped his son's forearm in encouragement as he passed him.

The mood settled and then a series of soft chords sounded from Felix Meyer's guitar. Around the room faces were smiling, and when Felix looked up and saw he was the centre of attention he blushed, mumbled a word of apology and rested the guitar against his chair.

'I sense the attention of some of us is waning, so perhaps we should have our supper now.' Michael looked at Cordula, who responded by standing and making her way to the door. The Vanguarders followed her in the direction of the dining room.

When everyone reassembled after supper Frank settled comfortably on the sofa, Anja next to him, then Cordula. A number of the Vanguarders had spoken to him during the break, introducing themselves and asking polite questions and putting him at ease. Several had surprised him by expressing admiration for his courage, alone in a foreign country and a foreign language, and at a time like this. He enjoyed this novel interpretation of himself and resolved to live up to it. But then thoughts of a suitable first sentence for Cordula diverted his attention.

Ollie Lippert, one of those who had spoken to Frank in the break, raised his hand and was invited to speak. 'The Holy Father says that many Catholics have gone over to the socialists. And he says that the causes are ...' Ollie read: ' "... the disordered passions of the soul, the sad result of original sin which has so destroyed the wonderful harmony of man's faculties ..." ' Ollie left a short gap and then asked: 'So all the problems come down to original sin. Is that what the Holy Father is saying?'

Jochen asked Ollie what *he* thought, but Ollie shook his head.

'You brought it up, Ollie. You must have some idea.'

'I don't have to say something just because you want me to, Jochen. I want to know what Michael thinks.'

Michael asked whether there was interest in including this topic in their future reading. Ollie said he would like that, and there were other supportive voices.

'We may need a priest to guide us on this question,' Michael added.

'Not Father Klein. We don't want him here.'

'You know the Vanguard is a male group, Anja,' Michael countered sternly. 'You and Cordie are our guests. You should bear this in mind.'

Frank could sense Anja slump in response to Michael's reprimand, but she was quick to reassert herself. She retrieved the hand Cordie had been holding, stood up and stumped out of the room, leaving behind a dull silence, the air sagging as if it had lost a vital ingredient. Cordula stayed sitting quietly for a time, then excused herself and followed her sister.

Slowly the threads of the discussion reassembled around the encyclical. Someone drew attention to what was said about individual freedom and the need for balance with the common good. Jochen complained that it was too abstract. Did the Holy Father say what they should do? Things could not go on as they were, there would be civil war. Michael did not interrupt and Frank thought he seemed distracted, as if a part of his mind had followed his sisters out of the room.

As the discussion continued the gaps between the hesitant questions and Michael's answers grew increasingly long, until Michael said it was time to finish.

The atmosphere lightened and Felix again took up his guitar. Yellow-covered song books that Frank had not noticed before appeared and pages were turned. Frank found the text but did not recognise the melody, so he silently mouthed the words.

After the singing there was a short prayer, then the meeting was over. Michael said they should be careful on the way home, they should keep each other company as far as possible, they should not make things easy for any trouble-makers.

Each of the young men came and shook Frank's hand. They also shook hands with each other and then stood in a queue to shake

Michael's hand. Frank could feel their togetherness, their underlying affection for each other despite the occasional sharp remarks, their gratitude for Michael's leadership. All this lifted his spirits.

Michael insisted on accompanying Frank back to St. Benedict's, but the journey took place for the most part in silence. Except at one point, when Michael said: 'Sometimes I can't find the right words with Anja. I hope you can help her.' Frank was taken aback by the thought that he might be of help where Michael could not, and he did not reply.

The neighbourhood was peaceful, there were no groups milling around, no shouts interrupting the still night, just occasional animal noises. But as the walk continued Frank felt a deep chill infiltrate his body. He wondered how he would cope with the winter, the snow and ice and wind that now began to sweep through his imagination. He braced himself inwardly in anticipation.

When they arrived at their destination the two companions stood quietly together. Eventually Michael said: 'I used to be close to Father Klein, but we have grown apart.' He gave Frank his hand, then mounted his bike and rode off. Frank turned back to the presbytery. Its looming shape in the darkness made a lonely impression on him, and he hesitated to go in.

Friday 21 October 1932

Michael Auer arrived at St. Agnes's on the edge of the old town shortly before eight o'clock in the evening. He had seen Father Schapp at his brother's requiem Mass and had spoken to him briefly, through the grief and disbelief at Lukas's death. Since then there had been telephone calls, but this was the first chance for a longer, face-to-face conversation. He was led to the presbytery's study, where the two men sat down.

'How are your parents, Michael? Can I be of help?'

'I worry about my father. My mother is stronger.'

'And you?'

Michael spoke softly, almost to himself. 'I should have stopped Lukas that day. A march through the heart of the workers' district. There was bound to be violence.'

'I did not know your brother well. But the few times I saw him I felt there was something he wanted to tell me, or to ask me. I made a note to myself to speak to him, but the opportunity did not arise. I greatly regret my inaction.'

'He had lost his faith, Father, and replaced it with idolatry.' Michael looked up. 'At first I thought it was to provoke, that in some way it was directed at me. But now I think he was sincere.'

'The prayers that will flow for Lukas will form a resounding appeal. God will not be deaf to this appeal. You must believe that.'

The telephone rang. Father Schapp motioned to Michael to stay seated and picked up the receiver.

As the telephone conversation proceeded, the priest for the most part listening, occasionally interjecting, Michael surveyed the room. The centrepiece was a large desk, the surface of which was completely submerged by signs of intellectual labour, pages covered in writing and books propped open. Crammed book shelves lined the walls on both sides, the contents showing no order that Michael could discern. There was a couch resting against one wall, and piles of old newspapers lay around, some on the couch, others in the far corner of the room, the latter reaching almost to the height of a man.

After replacing the telephone receiver Father Schapp spoke. 'My brother Clemens has heard from Catholic Party colleagues that there is a willingness at the very highest level to consider letting the Party fall, if this would facilitate a concordat between Rome and the Reich.'

Michael had his own contacts in Berlin and he had heard these rumours. He had done his best to dismiss them, but he was uneasy. He knew there were many in the Catholic Party who had lost faith in democracy.

'Is there anything we can do, Father? I could speak to our headquarters in Düsseldorf. Twenty thousand Vanguarders across the country. We could bring pressure to bear.'

'I doubt that will be necessary. Much as the Catholic Party might desire a concordat, it would never pay such a price.'

Father Schapp suggested a hot drink and he and Michael went to the kitchen and busied themselves with cups and boiling water, milk and ersatz coffee. They sat at the kitchen table.

'And Judith, Michael? I trust things are well between you?'

Michael set down his cup. 'She thinks it is time for us to marry. When the mourning time for Lukas is over. She says we have waited long enough, sacrificed enough.'

Father Schapp showed no sign of surprise. 'Perhaps she is right. You have known each other for so long, and you have pledged yourselves to each other and never wavered from this pledge. Perhaps it is not natural to postpone the final step of your union any longer.'

Michael was sitting up very straight, tall and thin and sharp, the light glancing off his glasses. 'I would have to leave the Vanguard, Father. I would no longer be a young man in our sense, although there are older ones than me in other groups. It would be hard for me to give it up.'

'The Church will find other ways for you to live your faith. Even if at present it is not clear what these ways might be. Pray about it, Michael.'

Michael sat quietly and tried to slow his mind, to hear what God might want to say to him, but he was distracted by thoughts of Lukas. He could see his brother, a brown shirt too big for the boyish shoulders, tightly-belted trousers ballooning around the thighs and knees before disappearing into long leather boots, swastikas in abundance, face and bearing full of conviction.

'But I'm not sure the mourning time will ever be over, Father.'

Wednesday 26 October 1932

The topic of Frank's talk to the class was the treatment of night in a selection of nineteenth century poems. He knew about the night, in theory. It was a contradictory but creative place of otherness, of fear, of peace, of dreams, of excess, this he had pieced together from various sources. While his experience of most of these things was sketchy, he liked to write about them. It was a form of preparation for fuller experience.

When he began, his voice sounded flat and uninspiring in his own ears and he felt at odds with himself. But gradually this feeling dissipated and he started to feel fully present and confident in what he was saying. He could sense the others being drawn in, setting aside any initial reservations, and he experienced a few moments of intense happiness. After the class a few of the others stayed behind to discuss his presentation, and he found himself leading a small group in animated conversation down the stairs and out into the sunshine. The group eventually dissolved and he was left alone, catching his breath.

The day had conjured up a ragged, fretful wind, but this did not dampen his spirits. He was looking forward to the mensa, the atmosphere and the food, which he thought was not so bad.

When he entered the refectory he saw Anja, Jak and Stormy at the usual table, talking and eating and gesturing. There was a fourth person with them but a little to one side, a broad figure with a square head and a narrow edging of dark beard.

Bill Parker was the newcomer's name. Frank was sure from just a few words that he was an American. A closer look showed that Bill had shadows under his eyes and his nose was disproportionately small. And there was something missing, an 'i' without a dot, but Frank could not put his finger on what it was.

Anja sipped at a hot cup. She smiled at Frank.

'The election,' Jak interjected. 'What'll happen this time?'

'Every few months, another election,' Anja responded. 'I'm tired of it.'

'I'm not sure you have that luxury.' Bill Parker was all of a sudden fully present in the group. 'Not under current circumstances.'

Anja shrugged her shoulders.

'You can't just be guided by your feelings,' Frank said. 'Your feelings might not be the right ones.'

'Feelings are just feelings. Neither right nor wrong.'

Jak got up and left, probably in search of what passed in the mensa for coffee. Stormy came to the rescue. 'What if I were to say I felt ashamed to be Japanese? Would you accept this or would you ask me why?'

Anja shifted in her chair and toyed with her cup. 'I suppose I would ask why.'

'And if I said it is because we Japanese are shorter than Europeans.'

'That's a stupid reason. Why feel ashamed because you're short? I'm not ashamed of my leg. It's not my fault. It's the polio.'

Frank looked at Anja, her chin jutting forward, trying to convince herself, he thought. It was the first time he had heard her talk about her leg.

Stormy looked at his plate and then at Anja and said, matter-of-factly: 'So you agree that feelings can be right or wrong.'

An eruption of noise threatened to drown out the last of Stormy's words. Frank looked to his right and saw a group of young men in brown shirts clambering onto a table, pushing trays and plates and cups aside with their feet. One of them raised the bull-horn he was carrying to his mouth and started to talk, turning his head and then his whole body to one side and then the other, encompassing the wide room. The mensa seemed to take a step back, to allow space for the young man's voice. At first the words were measured, but soon the pace quickened and the volume rose. The mensa suddenly surged back with jeers and taunts. Frank screwed up his face, trying to distil the speaker's words from the general clamour. He made out something about the hour of need, the abyss, resolve, purity, sacrifice. 'Typical Nazi Scheiß,' he could imagine Jak saying.

A cup flew across the room in the direction of the speaker but missed its target and crashed onto the floor. Other items followed, an increasing number finding their mark to laughter and applause, until it became an avalanche. The speaker carried on as best he could but one by one his companions jumped from the table until he was left there alone, using his bull-horn to ward off projectiles. Finally he gave up and clambered down, once or twice raising the instrument to his mouth and accusing or cajoling his tormentors.

A large group of students materialised from the surrounding tables and moved forward, surrounding the brownshirts. One of the group pointed to the mess of broken crockery and spilled food and drink on the floor and demanded that the brownshirts clean it up. Mops and rags were found from somewhere and thrust into their hands.

'They should sing,' a voice called out. 'Let them sing.'

There was loud acclamation for this idea, a banging of fists on tables and a stamping of feet on the floor, a chorus of 'sing, sing, sing, sing', and the brownshirts were pushed and pulled until they complied, hesitant and jerky and resentful. The mensa sat back and enjoyed the spectacle.

Jak had joined in the throwing, launching things he had picked up here and there on his return journey to the table. As he sat down his eyes were shining, his tongue constantly licking his fleshy lips. He looked at Anja and a broad smile broke across his face, drawing forth a responsive smile from Anja. Frank imagined that at any moment they might fall into each other's arms, and he felt a brush of jealousy.

'Not sure that's so clever.'

Bobby O'Donnell was suddenly there, bow-tie and knowing look, with one of the other Americans from the foreign students' night. 'Just a spectator, didn't you say Jak? Watch the flailing beast sink into the mud, with its poetry and philosophy and music. Almost word for word, I think.'

There was no response from Jak. Bobby turned to Bill Parker and said, in English: 'Billy boy, everything all right? Stomach full, body warm?'

Bill ignored the remarks. He said they should speak German, and Bobby cast his gaze ostentatiously around the table. 'I do apologise. Of course, Stormy. And the young lady? Is she one of us or is she a native?'

Anja looked away.

Bobby continued, addressing the table as a whole. 'I suspect our friends in brown have long memories. And I doubt that squeamishness is one of their characteristics. So I'd be careful.'

Bobby did not wait for a response. He left with a flourish, his acolyte in tow.

'Silly bow-tie,' Anja said. 'I think it looks stupid.'

Jak stood up suddenly and slung his rucksack onto his back. He said he was going to the club to play table tennis, but there was no sign of interest from the others and he headed for the door. Anja said she had a lecture and gathered her things and said her goodbyes, slightly modulating her words and gestures according to their target. Stormy and Bill and Frank took their time, ambling out of the refectory and down the stairs. There was a long bench with used books for sale in the foyer and Stormy detached himself and went to look at what was on offer, leaving Frank and Bill to walk outside together. The two of them stood blinking to adjust their eyes.

'Stay right away from that club of Jak's. It belongs to the reds.'

Frank felt a tremble of excitement. 'Is Jak a red?'

'Whether he is or not, stay right away. Especially now with the election. There'll be bloodshed.'

'But what would they want with me?'

As soon as the words were spoken Frank recognised their foolishness. He tried to retrieve the situation by gripping Bill's elbow and promising to avoid the club and to keep his wits about him.

The conversation ended with a warm handshake. As Frank headed on his way he suddenly realised that the 'i' without a dot was the lack of a moustache to accompany Bill's beard. An unflattering look, he thought, but fully in keeping with the distinctiveness he had sensed in Bill.

Saturday 29 – Sunday 30 October 1932

The Vanguarders were not long into the hike before Theo Lindner started to sing, of a wide open world and the yearning of youth.

Wir sind jung, die Welt is offen, o du weite, schöne Welt.
Unser Sehnen, unser Hoffen zieht hinaus in Wald und Feld.
Bruder, laß den Kopf nicht hängen, kannst ja nicht die Sterne sehn;
aufwärts blicken, vorwärts drängen, wir sind jung, und das ist schön.

The others joined in, each in his own time, until all were singing, vigorously and joyously in unison. Ollie Lippert was energetically beating a small drum, emphasising the rhythm.

Theo started a new song and a chorus joined him to pledge their souls to faith, honour and Fatherland.

Auf, ihr Brüder, steht zusammen darum fest mit Herz und Hand!
Laßt in unsren Seelen flammen: Glaube, Ehre, Vaterland.

When this song was finished someone called out a new title. Theo took the lead but this time the response was tentative. After a short while Theo let the song die away, leaving Ollie's drum beating in the emptiness. Another song was suggested, Theo made a start and this time the response was strong.

This pattern was repeated as the Vanguarders walked into the afternoon. Theo would start a new song and, if the response was enthusiastic, it would be sung through, often with repetitions. From time to time Theo would recapitulate one of the favourites and the group would relax into a vigorous rendition. Propelled forward by the music they covered the twenty kilometres to the camp site in three and a quarter hours, arriving just before five o'clock. The southside Vanguard group was already there and there were warm handshakes and introductions. Michael's group set about pitching their tents.

Frank had enjoyed the hike, even though he sensed his conspicuousness more than usual, with his knobbly knees exposed by the short pants that Michael had lent him, and with the silver grey shirt, also borrowed from Michael, dragging up under his armpits. He did not know any of the marching songs so his contribution was limited to some weak humming, but the atmosphere infected him as it clearly did his companions.

He appreciated not having to make idle conversation. For once he could be together with the others and by himself at the same time. And despite the constant noise the atmosphere was peaceful. The countryside seemed welcoming, thoroughly familiar and at ease with this sort of pageantry.

He had been surprised when Anja had told him the previous week about the hike and Michael's invitation to join. Anja herself had been dismissive. Boys afraid of growing up immersing themselves in their idea of nature while their mothers and sisters stayed behind and washed their dirty clothes, darned their socks and made their beds. But then she had gone on to list the things he would need. Sturdy boots, of course, and warm clothing, the nights were getting colder, a blanket and a change of underwear and wash things. Did he have a pair of pants that came to just below the knees? And long socks? That's what they all wore. And a silver grey shirt? Michael would lend him one. He should bring some sandwiches. And something hot in a thermos flask. There would probably be an old thermos lying around in Father Klein's presbytery. He would need to be at Anja's place at one o'clock on Saturday. Could he find his way there by himself? Did he have a rucksack?

Felix Meyer came and sat next to Frank. 'Michael says that you and I are to share a tent. Come on, I'll show you where we are.'

Frank had his right boot and sock off. He was examining a large blister on his toe, courtesy of the old boots he had borrowed from Father Klein. He did not have anything to bandage his toe with.

'We usually have a medical kit. I'll see if I can find it.'

Felix soon reappeared with a small bag containing bandages and antiseptic. He watched while Frank attended to his toe.

'I hope you don't snore. Last time I shared with Jochen and he snored the whole night. I hardly got any sleep.'

'At home I sleep in a room by myself. I don't have a brother, just two sisters. I don't know if I snore.'

'Tell me about where you live.'

Frank started to describe the beach at home, the rocks at one end, the waves crashing in and the spray flying, and dolphins, in and out of the water like bending shadows. But despite his own enthusiasm he could sense Felix's attention waning and he tried a different approach.

'And sometimes you can see ships on the horizon. I used to wonder where they were going.'

'I went to the Baltic once,' Felix said. 'The weather was overcast. The sea was like slate, flat and grey. One of my cousins got sick. We were supposed to stay for five days but we came back after only three. It was not enjoyable. And in one place the people on the beach had no clothes on. They were floppy and ugly.'

Frank let this confidence pass unremarked. He bandaged his toe, put his sock and boot back on and limped after Felix to the spot where they were to pitch their tent. They were the last, and Michael urged them to hurry.

—

Michael and Harald were of a similar age, closer to thirty than to twenty, significantly older than most of the others, and perhaps it was this which caused them to gravitate towards each other. At first they concentrated on eating and drinking. Then Harald asked: 'You were in the seminary?'

Michael swallowed a mouthful of tea. 'Only briefly. Or so it seems, in memory. But it was nearly two years.' He paused. 'The decision to leave had nothing to do with sexual things. I did not find that side of it difficult. It was just a feeling that I was not in the right place, that the person there was not really me.'

'And now you have the Vanguard.'

'We were all in the Young Men's Catholic Association and in the hiking groups. But we wanted something more, a stronger commitment to Christ. So Peer Scharenberg and Father Weidemeier established a Vanguard group in Düsseldorf, and we followed very soon after, together with Cologne. Now there are groups right across the country. '

'Father Weidemeier?'

'He is originally from the Saarland, but he has lived in Düsseldorf for many years now. He is a Jesuit, a scholar and a fine orator, a very gifted man.'

There was the sound of a striking match and the glow of a cigarette off to one side. Michael looked in the direction of the glow. He waited, then called for the cigarette to be put out. He turned back to Harald. 'One of our basic rules, but the others leave it to me to explain .'

'Everyone looks up to you, Michael.'

'You think I'm too dominant?'

'They need guidance and inspiration. They're still just boys.'

'And what are we?'

'We've stopped being boys. But we're still young enough to remember what it was like.'

'Sometimes I'd like to go back there. Then I remember that when I was there all I wanted was to leave it behind.'

Harald smiled. He left a few moments of silence and then said: 'I haven't properly expressed my condolences. I can't imagine...'

'Of course it's much worse for my parents. A good Catholic family, pillars of the Church. And a son, killed, marching with *them*.'

Michael looked around. The scene was one of blurring shapes and interweaving shadows, of soft voices and drifts of laughter. He continued, his voice even softer. 'Lukas told me that doubts about his faith had grown inside him until he could no longer resist them. He was frightened at first, without moorings, but then the fear disappeared and was replaced by a new love for Germany. He said he joined the Nazis out of love. I think he was sincere.'

'Harald.' Felix was walking towards them, carrying his guitar. 'Harald, come on. You brought your mouth organ, didn't you? We'll start soon.'

'Sorry Felix, I forgot it. I'm sorry.'

'Oh. That's too bad. Next time, then, Harald, I suppose.'

Felix rejoined an even younger-looking member of the southside group, also equipped with a guitar. The pair started to outline a familiar melody and a few tentative voices joined in, but most of the Vanguarders were still talking or eating or drinking or just sitting and a critical mass was not reached.

Harald said, his head down: 'I live in Jakob Lane. I heard gunshots that afternoon and I saw someone fall.'

The words drifted away into the peace of the evening and the gentle guitar chords and the murmuring voices. It took Michael a little time to respond.

'Lukas?'

'I did not know at the time.'

'You told the police what you saw?'

'I should have, I know.'

'But he was just a Nazi.'

'I don't know, Michael.'

'And now he is my brother.'

Harald was unsure whether these last words were a question or a statement. He waited, but Michael remained silent.

Felix and his companion were now playing with more authority. The singing began to gather pace and soon there were signs of a friendly rivalry between the two Vanguard groups, a battle as to who could pour the most of themselves into the words and the notes. But this competition soon settled and an equilibrium was reached that seemed to propel everything forward with a minimum of effort.

More than an hour passed before the collective enthusiasm started to wane. Then Michael got to his feet and thanked Felix and his fellow musician and said it was time for sleep. But first there would be a prayer.

The campfire was glowing more than burning. The young men huddling around it shuffled from their bottoms to their knees. A stillness fell over the group, then Michael started the prayer and the others joined in, uttering well-worn words that spoke of service and dedication and weakness and forgiveness. When the prayer was finished Michael said: 'Dear Brothers, Our Lord Jesus Christ gave his life so that we might live. Let us in the Vanguard dedicate our lives so that our German Fatherland might live again in truth and freedom as an equal partner among nations under God. I wish you all a peaceful sleep.'

—

At various times during the evening Frank's attention was drawn to the two figures sitting slightly apart from the rest and silhouetted against the fire. He wondered what was occupying them so intensely. He thought it might be the vacuum that, according to Harald, must be filled with good or it would be filled with evil. But evil seemed far away from this night and this place and Frank could not quite believe in it, so he tried to think of other possibilities. Then as he watched he saw silences growing and he hoped these were companionable and was relieved when the singing began and Michael and Harald were drawn in, any distance between them put aside.

The prayer that Michael chose when the singing finished was in its English form as familiar to Frank as breathing, but the candidly spoken German words and the surrounding hum of the night and the hush of the lake invested it with new meaning. And there was new meaning in Michael's words about the German Fatherland, which Frank felt were addressed to him as much as to the others. It was as if a second self had been added to his old one, a self that spoke a different language and inhabited a different history. He came away with a feeling of lightness and roominess, a sedate form of ecstasy, if such a thing were possible.

Later that night, as he lay in his tent with a grumbling stomach and cold feet listening to Felix's steady breathing, Frank tried to bring this new self into focus, to explore it, to justify his right to it, but he was not sure he could. He turned over and tried to sleep, but the weight of the enclosed space settled down on him and brought with it the memory of an earlier self. An ungainly boy of fourteen in a tiny tent in the backyard of his neighbour's house, a girl, relaxed in her young body, visiting her grandmother during the summer holidays, the boy and the girl drinking sticky juice from tiny cups and eating sweet biscuits, close to each other, the boy not sure what to make of the enthralling blur of sensation and emotion that was completely new to him. He had waited for her the next summer and the one after that, but she had not come again. Her name was Aileen, Frank spoke it out loud before he could catch himself. He eased himself onto his elbow and then settled back, grateful that Felix had not stirred.

—

Frank woke the next morning to a dare. You had to swim out to a buoy that was bobbing on the water about fifty metres from the shore of the lake.

A few of the young men were bending and dipping their hands into the water but no one seemed serious about venturing further. Then one of the southsiders appeared in swimming trunks and after a long run-up hurled himself into the water. He came up splashing and gasping for air, then propelled himself forward and began to swim. He was not very accomplished, every couple of strokes raising his head and shoulders well out of the water for breath and then crashing on, but he finally reached the buoy. There was a rousing cheer from his southside colleagues, sporadic applause from Michael's group.

Felix said: 'Frank grew up near the sea. I'm sure he could do it. For the honour of our group, Frank.'

Felix's animation at first amused Frank, but the single voice was joined by others in an insistent chorus. He protested that he did not have swimming togs, but was assured that this did not matter. 'No girls here,' someone said.

The southside hero was just getting out of the water and Frank was struck by his powerful physique, broad across the chest. Frank had the frame but insufficient flesh to do it justice. But for this challenge it did not matter. He knew he was a much better swimmer than the southsider.

He stripped down to his underpants and stood shivering. He was not going to perform a crazy dash into the water, so he walked to the edge and waded in. He had to grab for breath. He wanted to turn and go in backwards like he always did at home when the water was cold, it seemed somehow easier. But his underpants were sagging at the front. He pulled them up and took a few more half-steps. Then he took the plunge. The breath was dragged out of him and it took several strokes before it came again, in a series of short bursts. The water was not as buoyant as the ocean water he was used to and it was murky, he could hardly see his hands in front of him. But gradually his heart settled and he found a steady rhythm. Then he increased his speed and relaxed into his skill.

It must have been several minutes before he halted his progress. He began to tread water. The world was nearly at a standstill, his own movements reduced to a minimum. Through the quiet he thought he could hear light plopping sounds, as if tiny fish were darting their heads out of the water to appraise him. He felt a light nibbling on his skin and tried to shake it away before realising it was just the current playing with the hairs on his legs. He manoeuvred himself around to face the way he had come. He could see movement at the lake's edge and hear the sound of voices skipping across the surface of the water, and he imagined words of acclamation. He lay on his back and looked up at the sky and felt a moment of exhilaration.

Gradually he eased himself forward and began the return swim. It was only then that he remembered the buoy. He had forgotten all about the buoy. He felt his face begin to burn, despite the water.

Back on the shore Ollie Lippert was waiting with a camera, and he called to Frank to keep still. Frank instinctively put a hand in front of his crotch, simultaneously trying to broaden his shoulders as he smiled for the camera. There was a snatch of laughter and a trickle of applause, then the knot of watchers unravelled and Frank was left alone, blinking the water from his eyes.

When he got to where the others were congregated Frank was surprised to see a priest, putting on vestments for Mass. He looked to be of middle age, of average height and build, with a full head of closely cropped hair shot through with grey. He was smiling and gesticulating as he talked to Michael and Harald and some of the southsiders.

When the priest had finished robing he produced a white cloth from a large leather bag and spread it on a rock that was to be the altar. He withdrew two small candlesticks and other artefacts and laid these on the cloth. Finally he brought into the light a small covered metal container and gave it pride of place on the improvised altar. Then he turned and faced the assembly. He lifted his arms and held them open. The murmur of voices faded away.

'My dear young men. It is with great joy that I can be with you this morning in such a wondrous place, where God has called us to rejoice in His creation and His love for us. I would now invite you all to join with me in celebrating the Holy Mass, in which we commemorate the supreme sacrifice of the Cross, through which we are raised from our sins to Eternal Life.'

After the beauty of these introductory German words Frank found the familiar Latin of the Mass an anticlimax, but the fellowship he felt with those around him kept lifting him when his mind started to slacken. The rhythms of kneeling and standing, of listening and reciting and responding, gave him pleasure. He let his eyes drift to the water of the lake, where the sun's rays were being scattered willy-nilly. He blinked and turned back to the Mass.

The homily was devoted to the Reichstag election, just a week away. The priest reiterated the incompatibility of the teachings of

Christ with National Socialism, with its worship of false gods, its war against the Church. 'A vote for the National Socialists is not consistent with your duty as Catholics. You must ensure your families and friends understand this. No Catholic with any respect for himself or his Church may cast a vote for this party.' Frank could see in the stern faces and upright bodies of the Vanguarders a resolve to follow the priest's exhortation.

They entered the most solemn part of the Mass. Frank tried to focus, but he was feeling weak with hunger. His attention was caught by a snatch of birdsong. He raised his eyes to find its source but saw only sky. He tilted his head and with straining eyes made out a dark shape way up high, but he thought it was too far off for any sound it might emit to reach the ground. He was shocked out of his puzzlement by the sudden clanging of the altar bell. The bell rang again and his body shook at the dissonance.

After Mass a large tub of oatmeal was prepared for breakfast, with milk and syrup and dried fruit. There was also proper coffee. Frank savoured the feeling of repleteness returning to his body. Felix was sitting next to him and asked through a mouthful of food what he thought of Father Schapp.

'I liked his sincerity.'

Frank was hoping for additional information about the priest, whom he could see sitting with Michael and Harald and talking and listening energetically. But Felix changed the subject.

'Do you have a nationalist party in Australia?'

'Not like here.'

'We have communists too. Some of our Catholic workers have joined the communists, despite what the Church says. Do you have communists?'

'I don't know, Felix. I don't follow politics.'

Felix tore off some bits of grass and threw them gently in the air.

'Do you like Anja?'

'Yes.' Frank wondered if he should say more, but Felix left him no time.

'She puts me on edge.'

'But you like Cordula. The night of the Vanguard meeting you were playing for her.'

A voice called out that if Felix and Frank wanted to be in the tug of war they needed to hurry. But the two of them just sat there and watched as the others stretched and strained and collapsed in laughter and exhaustion on the ground.

'I always play for Cordula,' Felix answered after the delay, 'but I don't think she hears. Anyway, in the Vanguard we are not supposed to think about girls in that way. We should concentrate on the fellowship we have with the other boys. We need to become properly grown up before we can think of girls. The Vanguard is to help us become adults.' He added, in a lowered voice. 'But Michael has a girlfriend. Her name is Judith.'

The tug of war participants had recovered and had moved to a large open area of green further along the lake. Felix stood up and headed off to join them and Frank followed, wondering what Michael's girlfriend would look and sound like and whether Michael would change in some way when he was with her, become smoother, less edgy.

As they drew closer to the others Frank could see one of the southsiders demonstrating a throwing action to Father Schapp. But when the priest tried to put theory into practice the result was poor. The object he threw flew erratically and crashed into the ground a short distance away, to muted groans from the onlookers. Someone retrieved it, passing it to the instructor while everyone retreated to watch him demonstrate. This time the object glided gracefully into the air, spinning and arching upwards before curling and returning by an alternative path. Father Schapp took several short steps and put up his hands to stop its flight. There was clapping and cheering, mainly for the southsider's throw but partly for the priest's catch.

Despite his protestations Frank found the boomerang being pressed into his hands. He had once seen a demonstration of how the throwing went and he struggled to remember. Face into the wind and then turn so the wind is coming at an angle, hold the boomerang almost vertical, don't try to throw it too high or too hard. But there wasn't any wind. And he didn't know what grip to use, where to put his feet, what to do with his torso. His limbs felt stilted, everything in the wrong place. He held the boomerang out to the expert. 'I'm sorry.' The young man ignored the gesture. He used his hands to level Frank's shoulders, demonstrated where he should place his feet, drew back Frank's throwing arm, corrected the grip, rehearsed with him the movement of the throw a few times and then stood back. 'Breathe slowly,' the young man said. Frank felt a flurry of air come towards him but let it slide past, waiting for the right moment to announce itself. He tensed, moved his arm quickly forward, straightened his elbow and opened his hand. The projectile wobbled at first then gradually seemed to find itself and to begin to spin smoothly, to rise up from the ground, to cut through the air. Frank shielded his eyes from the sun. He saw the boomerang start to trace a curve and felt a rush of triumph but then disappointment as it stalled for no apparent reason and fell to the ground. Felix hurried off to retrieve it while Frank received the subdued plaudits of the others.

'Where did you get the boomerang?' Frank asked the southsider who had guided him.

'I made it,' came the answer. 'From an illustration. I'm aiming for the perfect throw. I'll stand without making the slightest movement and it will come to rest in my hands.'

'Good luck.'

The two of them shook hands. They smiled at each other. Frank almost shivered in the warmth of the exchange.

'Thank you,' the southsider said.

Felix was back with the boomerang and Frank noticed how strongly coloured it was, deep black, shining white, streaks of red and yellow. He took it from Felix and examined it more closely. He saw a depiction of three crosses mounted on a hill, a missal on an altar, other shapes that may have been representations or may have been background. The markings jarred, and Frank sensed that something distinctive had been carelessly appropriated. He felt a surge of protectiveness for his native land.

—

It was early evening when Frank arrived back at the presbytery. He was famished and went straight to the kitchen to prepare some food, but he restrained himself and did not eat as much as he might have. As always at the end of the weekend supplies were running short, and he wanted to ensure there was enough left for Father Klein.

Later in the evening he heard sounds from the kitchen and went to say goodnight. The priest was sitting at the table, together with the remains of a sparse meal. He gestured for Frank to sit.

'There was a priest there?' Father Klein asked.

'One came this morning to say Mass.'

63

'Father Schapp?'

'Yes, I think that was his name.'

'And Michael Auer full of confidence, leading the way?'

'I think everyone respects Michael.'

'We were very close once, Michael and I, before Father Schapp. But now it seems we are on different sides. I hope one day we can be reconciled.'

'Different sides?'

'Of the nationalist question.'

Frank remained silent, sensing he would soon be out of his depth.

'You may have seen a young man who comes to visit me,' Father Klein continued. 'His name is Ernst Tüchnow. I would like to introduce you to Ernst. He will be able to explain much better than I can the essentials of the nationalist movement, its inner truth.'

'But I thought the Church...'

'The Church is distracted by superficial things, by the rowdy elements and by the few who would misuse the movement for their own ends. But it will come round. Already at the highest levels in Rome there are those working for a rapprochement.'

'I don't really follow politics, Father.'

'This movement is more than politics. It addresses the depth of our being, just as our faith does. It calls on us to sacrifice ourselves for the greater good, the reawakening of our nation.'

'I don't think we have anything like this at home.'

'But there will be tumult, I think this is unavoidable. Be careful you are not caught up in it. Your father would never forgive me.'

'You should be careful too, Father.'

Frank was not sure why he said this or what he meant by it. He began to apologise, but the priest waved away the apology and stood to clear the table. Frank quickly got up to help.

'The Auers are a fine family, but the younger daughter is headstrong. I hope you will not allow yourself to be influenced by her.'

Frank felt a strong compulsion to defend Anja, but he was held back by a reluctance to burden his relationship with Father Klein. The rest of the tidying-up passed in silence.

Thursday 3 November 1932

It was a regular gathering now. Even on days when the first of the group arrived late the table was empty, waiting for them, a public acknowledgment of their friendship. They never commented on this. Nor did they talk about their reasons for gravitating to each other. Their conversations were not always comfortable. Anja would see to that, or Jak, or even Stormy. And sometimes they did not have much to say. But their silences were companionable and as they sat together they sensed a pooling of resources which strengthened them and sent them away with the assurance that they would return the next day, or the day after, for more.

'My dad has a business at home and he wanted me to join. Hauling business, based just outside Chicago. He started it with his brother, built it up from the ground. It's been pretty tough times back home these last few years. Not as bad as here but bad enough. On top of that my dad and my uncle had a disagreement a while ago and my uncle left the business. So my dad was very anxious for me to go in. But I wanted to go to college. He said fine, after college then. I said I wanted to study mathematics and he didn't see much point in that but he said okay. Then I finished college and said I wanted to come study in Germany. Well, he just about hit the roof. I said it would be just for one year. Then I asked for a second year and he said one more year and that's it. Now I'm into my third year.'

Frank felt that Bill's explanation was largely for his benefit and he was fascinated. In his imagination Chicago was a massive, sprawling place, full of fine examples of every kind of human achievement. For Bill to have left that behind and come here gave Frank confidence in his own decision. And for Bill to keep going despite his father's objections, that was brave.

'Chi-ca-go,' Bill said, with even emphasis on each of the syllables, as he turned to Jak and gave him a nudge. 'Stor-me,' he said, emphasising the 'me'. Frank caught sight of Bill's eyes and they both laughed. Jak just shrugged.

'But you must have universities in America,' Anja said, not understanding or simply ignoring the diversion.

Bill was serious again. 'We do, we sure do. In Chicago, a lot of good schools right there. But I heard about German mathematicians in my college courses. Riemann and Gauss and Cantor and Dedekind, the people we heard about. Right at the foundation of mathematics, rebuilding everything from sure and certain principles. I was really taken with that. So I thought I should come to Germany to study.'

Frank thought it must be wonderful to work on the foundations of something, and for a moment he felt frivolous.

'Most of the top mathematicians are in Göttingen, so I tried for there, but I didn't make it. Here they agreed to take me on. There are some good people here.'

There was a lull in the conversation. Then Bill said, in a lowered voice. 'You know Bobby O'Donnell was in Göttingen?'

Everyone was focused on Bill, except for Frank, who was watching Bobby at the far end of the mensa, holding court as usual.

'Physics is also very strong in Göttingen. Quantum theory, that's Bobby's field, the latest thing. His heart was set on working with the best, and he got in, a feather in his cap. But the top names had their favourites and Bobby never made it into the inner circle. So I heard from Charles Smith. After a year he'd had enough, so he left and came here.' Bill added: 'I think the whole thing is gnawing at him.'

'I don't feel sorry for him,' Anja said.

'Be careful of him,' Stormy said, his first contribution to the conversation. 'He would like you as a disciple.'

Bill shook his head, but Stormy went on. 'Charles Smith and Raymond Wright, always trailing along behind Bobby. Have you never wondered why?'

'They're all from Boston, I thought that was why.'

Bill smiled but Stormy would not be deflected. 'You have resisted Bobby's advances, so he uses other means. He sees an opportunity, and he buys your allegiance.'

A look of exasperation, or of defiance, replaced Bill's smile.

'I think I'm a match for Bobby O'Donnell. And I can't afford to refuse his help. If I did I'd have to go home. And I've come too far to go home now.'

Frank felt his mind quicken. He could sense in Bill's last sentence the prospect of a better understanding of his own motivation. 'What do you mean, Bill? Come too far?'

'Not too sure myself, Frank. It's just this country. Humanity's best and worst, it's right here, in spades, from one minute to the next. You feel you need to get to the bottom of it, and I'm not there yet.'

'Yes,' Frank said. He wanted Bill to go on, to delve deeper, to give examples, but Jak made a dismissive remark and Bill changed the subject. 'Anja says you've been unwell. Hope you're better now.'

'A lot better, thanks.'

—

The day after the hike Frank had woken with a fever and an aching body. That day and the next he had kept to his bed. It was Wednesday before his appetite returned.

Frau Wolters was in the kitchen, sitting with a hot drink. She asked if he would like something, then stood and busied herself with preparations.

'I hear from Father that you swam in the lake,' Frau Wolters said when she sat down again. 'That was nice and thoughtless.'

Frank was not sure why he had mentioned his swim to Father Klein. It was probably to break one of the awkward silences that were becoming increasingly common between them. Or to offer Father Klein the possibility that the hike was really a trivial thing.

'It was not so cold, once you got used to it.'

'Like my son. Won't be told.'

The woman breathed out audibly through her nose. She spoke to herself. 'God knows where he'll end up. Dead in some stinking ditch.'

Frank wanted to reassure Frau Wolters, to tell her that, from what he had seen, she had no need to worry about Max. But he anticipated too many complications.

'Is your country peaceful, Frank?'

It was only recently that Frau Wolters had started to use Frank's Christian name. He had taken this as a sign of a softening in her attitude towards him, of acceptance and even of affection. He had received this change with great relief. And he enjoyed the sound of his name in the woman's lilting accent.

'I suppose it is.'

'I don't understand why you've come here. Is it to gloat over us?'

Frank was taken aback. Then he thought guiltily of Jak in his front row seat. 'No, Frau Wolters, of course not.'

'It's true I haven't seen that in you. I've been watching but I haven't seen that. But why have you come?'

'Germany has a long history, I want to share in that. And I feel different when I speak German, more serious, freer somehow.' Frank felt his skin redden. 'I'm sorry, I'm not expressing myself very well.'

'You do well enough with your German, Frank. Well enough.'

Frank remembered his resolution to outdo Bobby O'Donnell in his command of the language. He was not sure he had achieved this, but it did not now seem to matter. Frau Wolters's acknowledgement of his competence, however subdued, was more important.

The woman stood up to clear the things from the table and she let Frank help her. 'Father Klein is a good priest, a good man,' she said. 'Not everyone sees that.'

'He has been very kind to me.'

'He is disappointed you don't go to Mass more often. He thought you would attend during the week but you only go on Sundays. He wonders if he should tell your father.'

Frank's parents sometimes went to Mass on weekdays, but he had always thought that Sunday was enough and he had not been put under any pressure. He said he was sorry that Father Klein was disappointed.

'Perhaps during the week you could go to Mass, a few times at least. It would please Father. Often there is no one there, just Father and the altar boy. And me, of course.'

Frank glimpsed an image of Father Klein and Frau Wolters and a featureless altar boy creating a sanctuary from scant materials in the early morning hush, and he briefly envied them.

—

The others had gone, it was just the two of them at the table, the mensa was almost deserted.

'I don't think anyone could make a disciple out of Bill,' Frank said.

Anja did not respond. Then she seemed to make up her mind. 'Has Father Klein spoken to you about what happened to my brother, to Lukas?'

Frank remembered the day after his arrival, Father Klein talking about the man and woman he had introduced Frank to at Mass. They were being sorely tested, but with God's grace they would be reconciled to the loss of their son. They would understand that he had not died in vain. The Bolsheviks must be resisted. They were intent on destroying the Church and subjugating the Fatherland.

'He said that he was brave and that he had died for Germany. He said you should all be proud of him.'

Something of the earlier look of disgust appeared on Anja's face. She composed herself.

'Cordie and I, we're both much older now. I don't know about Michael. He's always been old.'

Frank felt within himself a repeat of his reaction when he had first heard about Lukas, a sense of embarrassment at his own protected, unsullied world.

Thursday 24 November 1932

It was raining gently when Friedrich Auer dropped Anja and Frank off near the old town, just after seven o'clock in the evening. It was not possible to get the car down the narrow lane to the front of the building so they had to walk about a hundred yards. Frank had an overcoat with him and held it over both their heads. It was the first time he had ever done something like that with a girl, apart from his sisters.

During this manoeuvring Frank's mind was only half on what he was doing and where he was going. He was still occupied with what he had heard in the car from Herr Auer. The leader of the Vanguard movement was going to marry and Michael had been chosen as his successor. He would be moving to the Vanguard headquarters in Düsseldorf. Frank's response to this news had been enthusiastic, although he had immediately begun to wonder what it would mean for Michael's group in Siebenkirchen.

'Why didn't you tell me?' he asked Anja as they entered the building and began to climb the stairs to the second floor. But she did not answer. She was concentrating on accommodating her weak leg to the demands of the climb.

The front door of the flat was ajar and there was a hubbub inside. Frank wavered at the door but Anja went straight in. They were greeted by a middle-aged woman who smiled and said, in American-accented English, that she would take their coats, she would put them in one of the bedrooms, they would be perfectly safe there.

Anja was carrying a bouquet of flowers which she presented to the hostess, who received it with effusive gratitude. She took off her coat and handed it to the woman and then stood for a moment, letting the long velvety dress she was wearing settle against her body. Frank stared despite himself, slightly intoxicated by her slender but full form and by a sudden fragrant release of perfume. It took pressure from the hostess's hand on his arm to remind him that he too had a coat to offer up.

Bobby O'Donnell was quickly at their side. 'So pleased to see you both. And dressed for the occasion. I must say, Fräulein Auer, quite a transformation. And our young Australian, jacket and tie, trussed up like a turkey. How appropriate.' Bobby took a step back, to allow himself sufficient space to appreciate fully Anja's appearance and Frank's discomfort. Then he shepherded the pair into a large living room where at least thirty people were standing in small groups, drinking and smoking.

There was a record playing soft crooning music on a gramophone, but the predominant sounds were laughter and English conversation. Frank could feel Anja brace herself.

It had been two weeks previously that Bobby had swept up to the table in the mensa and declared with a flourish that the American community would be holding a Thanksgiving dinner and everyone, he had spread his hands to indicate the table's full complement, was invited. He had caught Anja's attention and spoken directly to her. 'Please do come. We need some local flavour and I think you'll do very well in that respect. And an additional feminine presence will be most welcome. We males do tend to dominate.'

Afterwards Bill had needed to work hard to assuage Anja's suspicions. She was not being teased or mocked, and if nothing else she would get an excellent meal.

'My father works in the city administration. He earns well and we have good food at home. I don't need charity from Americans.'

But she had finally relented. And now she took control and found a way through the crowd to a door leading into the dining area, Frank following. The room they entered was empty of people, but it offered two long tables with an impressive array of large platters. Anja went around lifting the domed covers, disclosing mounds of pale-coloured meat, potatoes, green beans, carrots, Brussels sprouts, mushrooms, rice, a scarlet-coloured sauce, stuffing, gravy. Frank whispered to Anja that perhaps they should wait until others showed interest in the food.

The door opened and, as if he were a regular guest with the run of the house, Jak burst in and in no time conjured a mountain of food onto his plate. Other guests started to come in and busy themselves with the food. Frank felt more comfortable, but his plate was only three-quarters full when he went back to the living room. He hoped this display of manners would not leave him feeling hungry later on.

The living room was set with two large square tables and a scattering of smaller rectangular ones, all sporting crisp white tablecloths. Bill Parker was there, speaking English to a group of people, none of whom Frank recognised. Stormy Weather had just come in and was in earnest discussion with the woman at the door. He seemed determined not to relinquish his coat, and while his German words appeared largely lost on the hostess his doggedness saw him through. Jak waved to indicate to him where the food was to be found.

Frank, Anja and Jak chose one of the smaller tables, Anja and Jak opposite each other, Frank next to Anja. When Stormy returned with his food he draped his coat over the back of the chair next to Jak and sat down. Bill came across and placed a half-empty glass at one end of the table to reserve his place. He smiled at Anja and tilted his head to show his approval of her appearance.

While Anja and Jak started to eat, Frank's attention was taken by a conversation at a neighbouring table. It was in American-accented English, and understanding it made Frank feel sophisticated and a little unreal, as if he had strayed off the street into a talking film. But while he could comprehend the words, the topics under discussion, a new deal, the end of prohibition, were only vaguely familiar to him.

As he was listening, Frank's gaze shifted to a smallish man talking to the woman at the door. The man was nearly bald, with just a half halo of grey hair, but he was slim and nattily dressed. He walked to the centre of the room, cleared his throat and began to speak.

'Ladies and gentlemen, if I could have your attention.' Again, American English. Frank saw a look of distaste on Jak's face. Stormy had a serene look that Frank attributed to satisfaction with the initial sensations afforded by the food. Anja was bent over her plate, her shoulders hunched in a posture of self-defence. 'My name is Morris Draper and I'm your host tonight, together with my wife Lucy, whom I think you all will have met at the door as you came in. I won't hold you from your food for very long, but I just thought I should say that you are all most welcome here. It is a great pleasure and an honour for us to host this dinner, and I would like to thank Bobby O'Donnell for making the suggestion.' Bobby stood and bowed, then gripped his hands above his head, like a prize fighter celebrating a victory. There was a short round of applause. The dapper man continued, still in English. 'As you will probably know, we've been going through very tough times back home, just like here, but we are going to have a new president with a new program and we think we'll be able to pull through and come into better times. So if I may propose a toast, ladies and gentlemen, if you would care to charge your glasses. To the United States of America, may she continue to prosper and grow and be a beacon of peace and freedom to the countries of the world.'

From what Frank could see Jak was the only one who did not stand and drink the toast, although Anja and Stormy were late to join in. When everyone had resumed their seats Jak lifted his glass and drained it.

Anja asked Frank what the man had said and Frank was just starting to explain when Morris Draper himself approached the head of the table and asked if the place was taken. He shook everyone by the hand, then sat down. 'Since I don't know any of you folks it would help me if you could introduce yourselves.'

Bill said: 'I'm sorry, sir, but apart from me, I'm from Chicago, and Frank here, who's from Australia, the others are not English speakers. Would you mind speaking German?'

Morris Draper made the change, quite smoothly. 'Please excuse me. I guess I thought, Thanksgiving, it would be in order to speak English. You'll see my German is a bit rusty. I spent two years here as a student, but it's been a long time. I'll do my best, but I'll ask for your indulgence. I'm a theology professor, here on sabbatical, trying to familiarise myself with the new German theologians. Now, tell me about yourselves.'

Each complied with some scant details about where they came from and what they were studying. For something to say, Anja volunteered that Frank was living with a Catholic priest and for that reason he might have some thoughts about theology. Morris Draper said that Catholic theology was foreign territory to him, he had quite enough to be going on with on the Protestant side. Stormy filled the gap that followed by saying he did not understand the divide between the Catholics and the Protestants. Surely what they shared was far deeper than what divided them?

'Well, Herr Ueda. Have I got your name right?' Morris Draper did not wait for an answer. 'Herr Ueda, we Protestants went through the whole Reformation to bring the Christian Church back to the Word of God in the scriptures and to free ourselves from all the accretions that had built up over the centuries. That you could only find your way to God through priests and their ceremonies. I think that's a pretty important difference right there. But I guess coming from Japan you may not be aware of all that.'

'My mother comes from a Christian family. I know something of the history of Christianity.'

'Well, you must excuse my ignorance. But may I ask, Herr Ueda, are you a Christian yourself? Do you believe in God?'

Lucy Draper appeared at her husband's right shoulder with a plate of food which she slid into place in front of him. She acknowledged the others with a wide smile. Her husband asked her to bring him a beer. 'In honour of our Australian guest,' he added, gesturing towards Frank.

'Some people believe in God,' Stormy said when the woman had gone. 'Others believe in country or race, or a leader. It's not so very different.'

Morris Draper sat up in his chair. He affected a jocular tone. 'Perhaps, on Thanksgiving, we should choose a less difficult topic.' His smile died before it reached his eyes.

'This is a shit country,' Jak muttered, looking up from his plate.

'Now look here,' Morris Draper said severely. 'There is no call for that kind of language. No call at all.'

The conversation stopped. Frank heard the sound of voices from elsewhere in the room roll over him. It was as if the gramophone had been turned off and the voices were rushing in to fill the void. But the music was still there, smooth and self-assured and suggestive of easy times.

Lucy Draper returned with a bottle of beer and a large glass. She encouraged her husband to eat. It would be a shame to let the lovely food go cold. Bill agreed, saying that it would soon be time for dessert and if they did not hurry along they might be sorry. For several minutes they all turned their full attention to the food.

When the flurry of eating abated Bill got to his feet, collected the others' plates, carefully scraped the leavings together and headed to the kitchen with a finely balanced load.

'Now that's good to see,' a voice called out. 'Bill Parker earning his keep as a waiter. Very laudable.'

Bobby O'Donnell's words, slightly slurred, were followed by a few threads of laughter. But the laughter lacked conviction and quickly died away.

Stormy continued his train of thought. 'Beliefs and doubts, they are just feelings. Feelings about what is true and what is false. They cannot be relied on. Only reason can be relied on.'

'I don't accept that,' Anja said abruptly. 'We should love and feel joy and sorrow. Relying just on reason would drain all the life from things.'

Professor Draper was quick to concur, saying that the young lady had put it very well. But his words were partially lost in the sound of chairs being pushed back and plates being cleaned and stacked.

Stormy pressed on through the disturbance. 'Revenge and jealousy and envy and hate. We would be better off without them.'

'I hate the Nazis.' Anja flashed a defiant look around the table. 'And I enjoy hating them.'

Professor Draper took a handkerchief from his pocket and wiped his forehead.

Bill had returned, carrying several plates with dessert, a pie and cream and pieces of fruit. He carefully laid down the plates then headed back towards the kitchen.

'Bill, my man, when you're finished there you might like to come and clear up this table. And a cup of coffee, if you wouldn't mind. We have the real thing, not the slops you get in the mensa.'

This time there was no laughter. A muffled voice told Bobby to leave it.

A few people were dancing at the far end of the room to some kind of swing music. Anja tugged at Frank's arm and started to get to her feet, but as Frank made to follow the record clicked a number of times to announce it was finished. The dancers returned to their tables and Anja sat down. Frank settled back in his chair, both relieved and disappointed and with a strong awareness of Anja's body beside him.

Somewhere there was a scuffle. Bobby O'Donnell was shaking himself free from Charles Smith's grasp and getting awkwardly to his feet. He waved an arm in Bill's direction. There was hardness in his voice. 'I'd like to say something about that young man. Gives himself airs and graces, he does, but doesn't have two cents to bless himself with. Daddy cut his allowance. So he came on his knees to me. Begging he was. Please help me Bobby. So I've been giving him some scraps from the table. Just so you all know. So I think he should damn well bring me my coffee like I asked.'

The room went quiet, apart from the occasional tinkling of spoons, the rasping of a throat being cleared. And a new song on the gramophone, about a railroad, a race against time. Frank could hear every word. 'Brother, can you spare a dime.'

Bobby sparked up. 'That's your song, right there, Bill Parker. Yes sir, right there.' But his laughter made a feeble impression and he slumped back onto his chair.

Morris Draper half stood and looked around, hands propped on the edge of the table. When he caught his wife's attention he said: 'I think different music, my dear. Not really suitable.'

Bill was suddenly directing a stream of English words at Bobby. 'I'll never accept another cent from you, sir. And you'll get back every last penny you've given me. I never want to talk to you again. You've shamed me and disgraced yourself. And on this Thanksgiving day.'

'It was the drink talking, Bill,' Charles Smith said. 'Just the drink.' Charles was trying to shepherd Bobby away.

Bill sat down and Morris Draper said to him, his short English sentences appearing to Frank like a small bird flitting from branch to branch: 'Take yourself a drink of that coffee, son. I'll be having a word to Bobby O'Donnell. And his father back home. I know the family. He'll be regretting this performance. You mark my words.'

Bill said nothing. Lucy Draper came and whispered in her husband's ear. He sat still, breathing heavily, then stood up and excused himself. There was a silence.

Finally Jak asked: 'What did Bobby say?'

Bill did not seem to hear the question, and Frank did not think it was up to him to explain. Then Bill got to his feet, took his jacket from the back of the chair and was gone.

'Bobby poked fun at Bill,' Frank said after a suitable pause. 'About lending him money. What he said was mean and low. Bill said he would have nothing more to do with him.'

'Bill should have hit him,' Anja declared.

An image of Bobby O'Donnell taking a blow to the chin came to Frank, and he let himself enjoy the spectacle. Then he listened as Stormy restarted the earlier discussion, as if nothing of note had intervened.

'I was exaggerating. Of course we cannot do without feelings. I was thinking of cases when your feelings tell you that something is true and your reason says it is not.'

The words were addressed to Anja, but she seemed to have lost interest. Frank took up the slack by asking for an example. Stormy thought for a while before responding.

'Many people in this country have been subjected, through upbringing and education and propaganda, these things are often hard to distinguish from each other, to the view that the Jews represent a danger to Germany. Their feelings tell them this is true, which means they believe it. But I think any sensible reflection will show that no such danger exists, at least to nothing like the extent to which it is claimed. So they should not accept that such a danger exists. They should not let their belief guide their actions.'

'But isn't that being insincere?' Frank asked. 'Not acting according to what you believe?'

'Sincerity is overrated. Many Germans are sincere in their racial attitudes. If anything it makes the problem worse.'

Frank was taken aback. He had always understood the attribution of sincerity to be a high form of praise. Something was wrong with Stormy's argument.

Suddenly everything was quiet. Frank looked up and saw that the room was empty. Then Morris Draper came in and cast an inquiring glance in their direction. 'Everyone's gone,' Frank whispered, and the friends sat at their table in a mixture of togetherness and embarrassment.

When they had made their way outside they divided as if by some natural process into two pairs, Jak and Stormy disappearing towards the centre of the old town, Anja and Frank heading back along the lane towards where Herr Auer would be waiting.

'We could help Bill with money,' Anja said through misting breath. 'I could ask Papa.'

Frank sought Anja's hand and she returned the pressure as they skirted the puddles that had formed along the way.

Friday 2 December 1932

The money from home had finally arrived and Frank hurried to the bike shop. He was relieved to see that the second-hand Opel he had set his heart on was still there, and he rode back to the presbytery with growing ease and a mounting sense of freedom. But his pleasure in his new acquisition was soon spoiled by a telegram from home, the flimsy envelope handed to him by Father Klein with a look of solicitude, bearing the news that his mother had been taken sick and was in hospital.

It was mid-afternoon and he rushed back to the old town. The man behind the post office counter directed him to a booth in the far corner. The enclosure was tiny and he could hardly stand up straight, so he leant against a side wall, railing inwardly at the blandness of the scene he could see through the glass, heavy women in thick coats addressing letters or affixing stamps to envelopes or standing patiently in queues. At one point the telephone gave a half ring but as Frank grabbed at it the ringing stopped. This happened again a few minutes later. Finally the telephone rang with assurance and he lifted the receiver, bent towards the mouthpiece and said hello. His heart lurched at the sound of an Australian-accented voice asking for the number he wanted.

It was Margie who answered, but their Aunt Claire quickly came on the line and explained that his mum had had a turn. His dad was at the hospital and they would know more soon but Frank should not worry, she was sure everything would be all right. After he replaced the receiver he was left with an ache in his back and a stomach full of doubt about his aunt's assurances.

As he emerged into the late afternoon sun the prospect of returning to the presbytery was suddenly unattractive. He wheeled his bike down to the river, in the vague hope that the sight and sound of moving water might soothe his mind.

He leant over the low wall that stood above the river bank and looked at the weeping willows dipping their branches into the water and at a row of punts secured to a small jetty. He could sense the facades of the nearby buildings staring down in a jumble of shades, the jaunty angles of their roofs complementing the range of their colours. He knew that the scene was peaceful and beautiful, but his anxiety overrode this knowledge.

It occurred to him that Jak might be at the club so he set off in its general direction. The cobblestones were difficult to negotiate and his initial progress was almost crab-like, but once he was past the old town the going was smoother. He glided through the dusk, past workers hurrying home and stragglers staring into shop windows or surveying political exhortations plastered on ubiquitous advertising pillars. Before long he was in front of the building, a narrow structure of two stories distinguishable from its neighbours only by an unruly pile of bicycles at its entrance. He had not yet bought a chain and lock so he carried his bike inside.

Jak was there, immersed in a table tennis game, and Frank felt his anxiety release. He sat on the floor, resting his back against the wall. His view was blocked by a group gathered at the side of the table but he did not mind. It was enough to be in the room with the others and to sense the ebb and flow of the game and share the innocent tension it created. He smiled to himself as a 'merde' came from Jak's lips. He dozed, then jerked awake. There was a smattering of applause. The game was over.

'A proper pub,' Jak said as he came up to Frank, bringing with him the sweet-sour smell of perspiration. 'Let's go.'

As they entered the corridor one of the office doors opened and a purposeful figure came out, almost colliding with them. Frank immediately recognised Max Wolters. He gestured a greeting, but Max took no notice. His attention was on Jak.

'There could be a raid,' Max said sharply. 'You should get out of here.'

'Why tonight?' Jak asked, but Max did not answer. He disappeared into the games room, where he could be heard issuing instructions.

Jak stood still, seemingly undecided whether to stay or go. Then without a word he headed for the front door and out into the early dark, where he grabbed his bike and set off at breakneck speed. Frank followed in desperate pursuit, fearing disaster at any moment, for Jak or for himself and for any of the shocked pedestrians who weaved out of their path. But they arrived unscathed.

The pub Jak had led them to was not far from the main mensa. It was small and low-ceilinged, almost claustrophobic, but passably lit despite an abundance of cigarette smoke. There were groups playing cards and one table was hosting a game of chess. Jak had left his bike unlocked, propped against the building, but Frank carried his bike inside and asked the man behind the bar if he could put it somewhere. The man pointed to a spot next to the door. 'Don't make a habit of it, mind,' he said as Frank thanked him.

Jak needed several trips to deliver everything he had ordered. The last part of the consignment was a plate piled high with onion tarts, and when confronted with these Frank found to his surprise that he had an appetite and he wolfed down several in a blur of pleasure. He raised his beer mug, a garishly decorated thing with a prominent handle that Jak said he should grip in a full fist, and washed down the leftovers with a long swig. He found himself unpleasantly surprised by the beer's distinctive wheaty taste, but hoped it would grow on him.

'Will the Nazis come?' Frank was hunching forward, almost whispering.

Jak answered through a mouthful of onion tart. 'They'll come. It's just a matter of when.'

Frank let this thought settle. Then he asked: 'How long have you known Max?'

When Jak was ready he answered a different question. 'We live in the same building, same floor.'

'He's not a student, is he? He's too old.'

'He's a worker and a communist. And he's the only one who can give me a proper game of table tennis.'

The conversation stalled. Jak was looking around as if he were expecting someone. To maintain the momentum Frank asked: 'Where do you think Bill's got to?'

'Bill has contacts. He'll be all right.'

Frank was already near the end of his second bottle of beer and felt light-headed. He waited for the sensation to pass and then went to the bar and ordered more onion tarts. When he sat down it took him a few seconds to regain his equilibrium.

'You should slow down,' Jak told him.

Frank looked towards the door to make sure his bike was still there. As he watched someone brushed against it and the bike wobbled and swayed and then settled back in its place. He breathed out heavily. He looked at Jak and said he needed a leak.

'Down the lane, at the end.'

When Frank got outside the cold slammed into him. He hugged himself for warmth then edged his way into a narrow laneway and followed it, one hand feeling along the side of the building until he came to the toilet. He went into the stinking dark and completed the task as quickly as he could.

When he got back inside he was stunned to see Stormy Weather sitting at the table, a bottle of beer in front of him, talking to Jak. Frank flopped into his chair and tried to hide his surprise.

The three of them sat there, drinking their beer, finishing the tarts. Jak and Stormy occasionally spoke to each other, mainly about Bill, what they could do to help, but Frank did not try to join in. He told himself he was drunk. The pub was noisier now. He noticed the chess players had gone. He was anxious about his bike. He kept looking up to make sure it was still there, still upright.

The eating and drinking finished and through a series of stumbles and lurches Frank made his way outside, assisted by Jak and Stormy, the latter wheeling his bike for him. Somewhere along the way two female figures became attached to the group and soon they all entered an unremarkable building. There was a space near the front door and Frank was told he could wait there.

The others disappeared up the stairs, in silence apart from their echoing footsteps. Then one of the women reappeared with a wooden chair. There was a cushion that she used her hands to puff up. She invited Frank to sit and he followed the invitation. His bike had found its way inside with him, and he rested his hand on one of the mudguards. A draught came from somewhere and he pulled his coat more tightly around his shoulders. He hoped the other two would not be long. He knew what they were doing.

The door opened and a woman came in from the street. She stopped and stared. Frank's bladder had started to pressure him and he spoke first. 'I need a toilet.'

'You're drunk.'

'My friends left me here.' His hands were pressing his abdomen. 'Please.'

The woman signalled to follow her. 'But if you make any trouble, I have friends here, I'm telling you.'

Frank struggled to his feet and started to climb the stairs. Then he remembered his bike and stumbled back to get it. By the time he looked up the woman had disappeared. He called to her but there was no reply. He started to climb, the stairs were steep, he needed to concentrate on his feet and his bladder. A wheel of the bike banged into the wall then on the rebound against his shin. He swore. The woman was waiting for him on the landing. She helped him to steady the bike and he thanked her.

He was desperate by the time they got to the flat. The woman opened the door and pointed the way. He started to wheel his bike before letting it fall to the floor in a final rush to his goal. He did not bother to close the door properly before dropping his pants and freeing his penis and letting the pressure go, eyes closed when he found his range. Then he quietly closed the door and put the toilet seat down and sat on it. The empty bladder felt good. There was a snatch of nausea but it gave way to a moment of peace. But this was interrupted by a knocking on the door. 'Hurry up. I need to use it.'

Frank washed his hands at a tiny basin and splashed water on his face.

'I'll be quick, so don't think about taking anything. In fact, you stay outside the door and walk up and down so I'll know where you are. And recite something.' The woman pushed past Frank and closed the toilet door. He noticed she was carrying her handbag.

He moved away and then stopped. He felt foolish. 'I can't hear you,' came the woman's voice, and Frank started to recite. His choice was an English poem, he was not sure why, a night poem, describing a place of beauty, of grace, of goodness and innocence. As he spoke the words he thought of Felix, playing for Cordula.

The recitation was word perfect, by the end a proper declamation, but it did not fully mask the sounds of urination coming from the bathroom. He was relieved when he heard the toilet flush and saw the door open.

The woman went up to Frank and put her hands in the pockets of his coat. 'Just to make sure,' she said. 'Please empty your jacket pockets. And the pockets of your trousers.'

Frank put his hand into his trouser pocket and felt a bundle of banknotes. He had forgotten about the money. 'I withdrew this from the bank. My mother is sick. I had to telephone home. I didn't know the cost.'

The woman stood near Frank and surveyed the things he had laid on the table, a handkerchief, a key-ring with a single key, a flimsy piece of paper with a handful of typed block letters, a packet of cigarettes and a box of matches. She touched each item, even the handkerchief, with a finger. She had taken her coat off and he could see a nice figure, tall and slim with a full bust. But she was not young, probably over thirty.

'What sort of friends would leave you just sitting there?'

'I drank too much and couldn't ride home. It was my fault.'

'I'll make herb tea. You'll feel better.'

Frank bent down and picked his bike up and found some space against a wall and gently rested it there. He went towards the woman, who handed him a cup of hot liquid.

'My name's Renate.'

Frank took the cup and held out his free hand for her to shake and said his name.

'What's wrong with your mother, Frank?'

The tea was hot and almost burnt his mouth.

'I got a telegram from my father. This afternoon.' He wondered whether that was right. Or was it yesterday? 'He said my mother was sick in hospital. He said to pray for her.'

Frank was holding the cup in his lap. He looked around for a place to put it but could not find anywhere within reach. His hands were shaking, the liquid close to spilling. The woman stood and took the cup and put it on the floor.

She said: 'If you would like me to comfort you it will only cost ten marks.' She put her hand to her blouse and started to undo the buttons.

Frank swallowed, he could feel himself stiffen, beyond his control. The woman moved closer. 'Come on,' she said, and helped him to his feet.

Frank was suddenly almost sober. He shook himself free and muttered an apology and began to collect the contents of his pockets. As the woman looked on in amusement he grabbed his bike and stumbled his way out of the room and down the stairs.

—

When he had left the old town behind and the traffic had thinned out he felt more comfortable and steered into the middle of the road. He sped up and relived for a few moments the ride with Jak, he ran the bike's front wheel back and forth across the tram tracks and let the bits of light reflecting off the tracks play against his eyes. But the front wheel caught in the track and when he tried to free it the bike twisted and he lost control and found himself tipped onto the hard surface of the road. He was shaken, but he thought that was all, a graze or two. His overcoat had taken the brunt of the fall. He was lying there, thinking which part of his body he should move first, when a pair of shadows fell across him. A voice said that he could not stay there in the middle of the road. Another voice said that he was probably pissed, and it served him right.

Hands helped him to his feet. He reached for the bike, stood it up and examined it, then cursed in English. 'Shit, the front wheel. Shit. I just got it.'

'Hey, this is Germany. Speak German, hey.' Frank felt unfriendly pressure on his chest.

'Leave him, Arnie. I know him. He's staying with Father Klein.'

'Looks like Pinocchio, doesn't he?' There was a burst of unruly laughter.

The one who had recognised Frank told his colleague to carry on without him, he would catch up. Then he extended a friendly hand in Frank's direction. 'Ernst Tüchnow,' he said. 'I'll see you home.'

As they walked, at first saying little, Frank stole occasional looks at his companion. Even in the dim light he saw an impressive figure, tall and lithe with a fine silhouette that was vaguely familiar, from the mensa or from Mass. He felt himself ungainly and dowdy with his scuffed coat and grazed hand, wheeling the bike with the buckled front wheel off the ground. When Ernst said that he knew someone who could fix the bike, he could come to the presbytery on Sunday after Mass and take him there, Frank could only mumble a few luke-warm words of thanks.

The presbytery was soon in view and Frank stopped and searched his pocket for the key. Ernst rested a hand on the bike and said quietly that Father Klein was a fine man and he would very soon be proved right.

'He's been good to me,' Frank responded. He found the key and made to move on, but Ernst held him back.

'There are reactionary forces in the Church who want to exclude our movement, but they won't succeed. Father Klein has told me that in Rome there is support at the highest level for our struggle against the Bolsheviks. The intransigents will be pulled into line.'

'I don't really follow politics.'

'I could take you to one of our meetings. There are some foreigners among us, some from the university.'

'I don't know.' Frank gave exaggerated attention to manoeuvring his bike inside the presbytery, and Ernst helped him.

'After Mass on Sunday then,' Ernst said, letting go of the bike. 'Gerd will have it fixed in no time.'

Monday 5 December 1932

Jak had his knee on a chair and was craning his neck to see what was happening. 'Bobby O'Donnell is showing his true colours,' he said.

Anja looked up from her food and followed Jak's gaze. She stood up, pushed her chair aside and set off towards the far corner of the mensa. Neither Stormy nor Jak said anything but they both got up and followed, dragging Frank along in their wake.

'A coward, humiliating Bill. And now sitting with these shits, in your stupid bow tie.' Anja was standing and trembling and waiting.

Bobby O'Donnell, flanked by a blur of brown shirts, responded. 'Your fervour was amusing to begin with but it's beginning to pall. Why don't you take your guard of honour and make yourself scarce, there's a good girl.'

'Hey, there's Pinocchio.'

Frank recognised the loudmouth from the previous Friday night. He surveyed the others. All nondescript, except for Ernst, who was sitting quietly, eyes downcast, the barest hint of a smile around his mouth.

'Flat on his arse he was. And pissed as a parrot, weren't you Pinocchio?'

'Pinocchio. That's excellent.' Bobby reached out and flamboyantly shook Arnie Wriedt's hand.

Stormy Weather made eye contact with Bobby and calmly asked if he really wanted to throw in his lot with these people.

'Why don't you piss off back to your own country, flat face?' a voice said. 'Germany is for us Germans.'

'No need to be crude, young Gerd,' Bobby intervened. 'Our friend Stormy Weather is a beacon of Western culture, despite his facial features. Germany is the richer for having him here amongst us. I dare say you could learn a lot from Stormy.' He looked Gerd's lumpy body up and down, paused for effect, then said: 'Perhaps not.'

Gerd crumpled back into his chair and Bobby continued, his words flowing freely. 'And we Americans, we are also a useful addition to the mix. The spice of the new world. And Pinocchio, a whirlwind from the south seas, full of wiry innocence. And Jak our Celtic warrior, master of table tennis and surliness and ladies of ill repute. All useful ingredients. In small measure, of course, just a little leavening.'

As Frank watched this performance he saw Bobby glance surreptitiously in Ernst's direction, and it was suddenly clear to him that the whole speech was for Ernst, that Bobby was desperate for Ernst's approval.

Stormy touched Anja lightly on the arm and she turned on her heels and led the group back to their table. As they approached they saw that, as if put there by magic, Bill was in his usual place, a bowl of soup sitting untouched in front of him. They acknowledged Bill's presence as they sat down, although nothing was said.

Frank did not want the conversation to return to the events of the previous Friday night, so he asked: 'What does Bobby see in them?'

There was no answer to Frank's question, just a few glances at Bill. Then Anja addressed herself to Jak and Stormy. 'You went to Heldstraße?'

Jak shrugged. Stormy commented that when you are thirsty you should drink, and Anja replied that she supposed it was none of her business. Frank stifled a laugh and muttered something, not really under his breath, about a busybody. Anja shook her head at the nuisance of his interjection.

After some further desultory conversation Jak nudged Bill and said he had an idea that might interest him. He put a hand in his pocket and produced a plain envelope. Anja picked up the envelope, looked inside, then handed it straight back to Jak. The others went on with their eating.

'Earn some money,' Jak said as he slid the envelope across the table. Bill took his time. He let the contents slide out and glanced at them.

'Not bad, eh?' Jak went on. 'I can get them for thirty pfennigs each, twenty for five marks. Up to us what we charge. At least forty pfennigs.'

Anja took one of the pictures which she turned the right way up and examined. She nudged Frank, who had been trying to avert his eyes. 'She has beautiful breasts. I wish my breasts were as beautiful as hers.'

Frank glanced at the photograph but did not say anything. Jak asked if he would like to see more but Frank shook his head. Anja picked up another picture and looked at it in silence.

'I'd had too much to drink, Bill. No hard feelings I hope.' It was Bobby O'Donnell, stretching a hand across the table in Bill's direction. But before Bill could react Bobby's gaze registered the photographs and the hint of meekness in his voice gave way to the customary sarcasm. He withdrew his hand.

'I do declare, smutty pictures, and at this table. The centre of righteousness, of probity and virtue. It seems our comrades in brown are on the money. A thorough clean out of the stables is needed.'

Bobby took a half step back from the table and directed his gaze at each of its occupants in turn. 'Jak of course doesn't surprise. But Stormy, Bill, Pinocchio, who would have thought? And the edgy young lady with the sharp tongue and the rollicking gait, so keen to defend a friend's honour. Looking to see what might have been, my dear. Dreams, dreams, where would we be without them?'

The table was silent, on the back foot. Jak was the first to recover. 'Like to buy? Fifty pfennigs each.'

'Thank you, Jak. But I prefer the real thing, and I feel it's beneath me to pay. Unlike you, I know.'

'Jak's joke. Trying to embarrass us.' Bill did not sound convinced by his own words.

'But Bill, we all know you are quite capable of embarrassing yourself without help from others.'

'That's ironic, coming from you,' Jak intervened. 'Surrounding yourself with Nazis.'

Bobby was quick to parry this attack. 'I think they'll make for interesting times. And you can hardly come all high and mighty with me. Just here to see the ship go down. Said so yourself, often enough. Or is that just playing to the audience?'

'You'd know all about that.'

'That's as may be. But I like to think I perform with a lightness of touch that is beyond you. Blundering about the place like a wounded animal.'

There was a suggestion of smiles between the two but the niggling tone made Frank uneasy. He thought he should say something to return the focus to Bobby's apology. But at the same time it was fascinating to watch this pair peeling layers of pretence from each other.

Stormy Weather said quietly to Bobby: 'When they clean out the stables, what makes you think you will not be among those who are swept away?'

'Stormy, an excellent question. And you know what? I can't be sure.' Bobby was leaning forward with his hands on the table edge. Frank could feel the warmth of his breath and smell the aftermath of his lunch. 'There'll be nothing prim or prissy about it. They'll be cutting through things in swathes.' Bobby stood up straight and made a sweeping motion with his arms. Like someone cutting tall grass with a scythe, Frank thought. 'And I'll just have to keep my wits about me. Nimble and quick. I like to think that's a strength of mine.'

'Why not ask your friends for a brown shirt?' Jak asked. 'You could dress the part.'

'Perhaps I will. But, you know, a few scraps of clothing won't save you if you're foolish or unfortunate enough to be in the path of the leviathan when its temper is up. Nothing will save you then.'

Bobby assumed his full stature, clicked his heels, paused and then for an instant raised his right arm in a Hitler greeting. He laughed, from embarrassment or to reassure himself, it was not clear. Then he nodded in the direction of Charles Smith and Ray Wright, who had been standing quietly in the background and whose presence Bobby seemed to have somehow divined, and together they headed for the exit.

Bobby's performance left the mood of the table subdued and Bill and Jak and Stormy soon gathered their things and left. But Anja held Frank back. She wanted to know what had happened in Heldstraße, she knew the street's reputation. She poked and prodded and Frank tried to fend her off with an abridged version of his brush with this street. But he felt himself failing to convince her of his innocence, so he focused on diversion. 'I got a message on Friday that my mother was sick. I was worried all weekend. But there was another telegram this morning saying she is much better. On the mend, my dad said.'

Sunday 18 December 1932

Anja knew a restaurant in a nearby village that served good lunches. It was an easy bike ride away, and they had agreed that Frank would come to the Auers' place at midday. He was looking forward to spending time with Anja without the constant press of other people, and he hoped they would be able to resume their relationship from the point they had reached before Heldstraße.

They did not start to ride immediately, instead wheeling their bikes back in the direction of St. Benedict's before turning off the asphalt street onto a dirt path which travelled uphill, away from the town. The houses started to thin out and finally disappeared altogether. After a few more minutes a donkey came into view behind a dilapidated fence. As they got closer the donkey came to the fence to greet them, and Anja took a carrot from her pocket and let it eat from her hand. Some remains fell on the ground and the animal snuffled them up. 'This is Marie,' Anja said. 'I often come up here. I think we understand each other.' She ran her hand down Marie's long head, light brown with a white patch around the nostrils and mouth, then laughed as the animal pulled away from her attempt to fondle its ear. Frank handed her back her bike and they went on.

When they got to the top of the hill Frank looked down at the town. He could see the river and followed its course to the cathedral and the monastery, which now housed the theology faculty. He could not see the market place but he could imagine it, settled in behind the visible buildings.

Across the river was the railway station. He remembered the day just a few months earlier when he had left that dull old building, lugging his suitcase with a hollow feeling in his stomach and legs, and felt a sense of satisfaction with the progress he had made. When he turned back he saw Anja watching him. They shared a smile of complicity.

They mounted their bikes and started to glide down a gentle slope. Then the land levelled out and they rode in single file. Anja shot ahead but Frank sped up and soon was right behind her, wheels almost touching. He calmed his exuberance.

Anja signalled to stop. They came to a halt next to a stone column with a sloping roof, under which a crucifix was mounted. Anja dismounted, limped a little way into the field and picked some wildflowers, which she arranged in front of the shrine. 'It's a tradition, Frank. I don't suppose you have anything like this.' Frank felt a momentary irritation at Anja's presumption, but said nothing.

It was not long before the village came into view, first a cross on a steeple then one or two dark brown roofs, then half-sized trees, shorn of leaves, forming a wall of sorts. They came to a junction and turned into a narrow bitumen road. It was quiet, no vehicles on the road and no one out walking. They were in the village before they saw any signs of life.

They got off their bikes and went past a gate in a high archway. Frank stretched his head to see what was inside, he thought it might be a school. He caught faint smells of animals and earth. They turned into a short lane and Anja pointed to the restaurant. They rested their bikes against the wall and Frank took out a chain to secure his bike, but Anja shook her head to say it was not necessary.

A man greeted them as soon as they were inside, but Frank only understood a part of what was said and felt a small upset at his failure. They hung their coats and hats on pegs near the door and were led to a table near a window.

'It wasn't so cold, once you got going.' Frank looked around, enjoying the feeling of the extremities of his body returning to life. 'It's nice here.'

'We'll have stew. There might be rabbit in it. And I'll ask for mulled wine. And bread.'

While they waited the restaurant began to fill up and Frank strained to pick up pieces of conversation. He detected different cadences from those he had become used to, and sometimes there was a short delay between his mind registering the sound of a word and recognising its meaning. Anja asked him what he was smiling about. 'You think they're country bumpkins, don't you?' Frank saw a middle-aged man at a nearby table glance in their direction.

'No I don't.'

The food was delivered by a strongly-built woman, the owner's wife, Frank assumed. Two large bowls of stew, carrots, parsnips and potatoes he recognised at first glance, two cups of mulled wine, deep red against the white of the cups and two large pieces of bread, each with a knob of butter in one corner. Frank thanked the woman and received a forced smile for his trouble. The woman muttered something as she left, and Anja was quick to notice Frank's lack of comprehension. 'She asked me where I found such an odd looking creature.' She rested a hand on Frank's. 'We're not second best Frank, not to each other. We should never think that.'

'Of course not,' he said, avoiding Anja's eyes and hoping she would not pursue the subject.

They ate in silence for a few minutes and then Anja asked him about his mother. He said there was no more news. He had tried to telephone again but the post office had not been able to get a connection. They had told him it was very complicated. There had not been another telegram so he was not worried.

Anja took a sip of the mulled wine. Her face was flushed.

'What you said about Heldstraße. I don't believe you.'

Frank felt a stab of anger. 'I told you what happened.'

'Keep your voice down.'

They sat for several moments at odds with one another. Then Anja said she had something to ask. She had put aside her knife and fork and lit a cigarette. She mumbled into an exhalation of smoke.

'What are you talking about?' Frank's whisper was the sort which finds its way into every available part of a room.

'I want to go to bed with you,' Anja repeated. 'I have a condom. It will be perfectly safe.'

'But what about your parents?' Frank stammered. He remembered his father's words about temptation. 'The Church?'

'Were you thinking about the Church or your parents? In Heldstraße?'

'Anja, please stop!'

Anja energetically stubbed out her cigarette. 'Don't you want to touch my body?'

Frank glanced around the room. No one seemed to be paying them any attention. 'Why are you suddenly talking like this?'

'Because it's pointless asking any of the Vanguarders. If they so much as look at a girl in that way it's a black mark in their copybook.

So that leaves you. And I like you, Frank. I think it will be nice, the two of us.'

Frank was grappling for words. He rehearsed the German expressions he had available, but they seemed detached and unreal. Anja went back to her food and Frank waited. He knew that more was demanded of him, but all he could do was state prosaically that Michael had a girlfriend, perhaps some of the others did as well. But Anja would not be diverted. She said she did not think Cordie had slept with a boy and she wanted to be first. 'We could ask Bill if we could use his room. I don't think he would mind. And I think he would keep it secret.'

'Bill's religious. He wouldn't agree.'

'He needs money, we could pay him. I have money.'

The woman came and took their plates. Anja asked if she had any coffee but was told only the usual stuff.

When the woman had gone Frank started to relax. He looked at Anja and let the prospect she had opened up play wordlessly across his mind, and he felt his body sharpen in anticipation. 'We have plenty of time,' he said without thinking.

The restaurant was emptying but Anja was in no hurry to leave. She sipped her ersatz coffee and asked about Michael's Vanguard group. She prompted Frank by naming each of the members in turn and the two of them found themselves contending for the wittiest or most outlandish description of strengths and weaknesses and possible futures. But when it came to Jochen Anja put aside the levity and said that he had spoken enthusiastically about Frank's swim on the hike. He had said that water was Frank's natural element.

Frank was not sure if this was a compliment. 'I don't know what to make of Jochen.'

Anja replied that Jochen liked to test himself against Michael, but it was an unequal battle and he would never win. 'He knows this, but won't accept it. So he continues to push and pull. But you should not worry about Jochen.'

Anja started to get ready to leave, then hesitated. 'I've never learned to swim properly, Frank. Will you teach me, when the summer comes?'

Frank said of course he would. Then he realised that when the summer came he would be gone.

Saturday 24 December 1932

Frank was woken by a creaking sound outside his window. He pushed himself onto his elbows and listened. Nothing at first, then further creaking and tearing. He checked the time. Not yet six o'clock. He laid his head back on the pillow. At regular intervals he heard the noises repeating, although at a greater distance. Then he heard Father Klein's footsteps heading towards the kitchen. The priest would be leaving soon to say morning Mass. Frank would wait until he had gone and then go out and explore the sounds.

As he lay there his thoughts turned to the coolness that had entered the presbytery during the preceding weeks, hand in hand with the encroaching winter. At first he thought the cause might have been what he had told Father Klein in the confessional, but he doubted that his unremarkable list of sins could produce such an effect. As he reflected he became increasingly sure that it had to do with the Auers. Father Klein was engaged in a battle for their allegiance, and he had placed Frank in the enemy camp. Perhaps it was Frank's closeness to Anja, which he knew Father Klein had begun to suspect. Or his involvement with Michael's Vanguard group and the assumed influence of Father Schapp. Whatever the reason, the resultant loss of the modest companionship he had enjoyed with Father Klein had left Frank feeling queasy and adrift.

He must have gone back to sleep and the sky had already lightened when he finally stepped out into the sharp cold. He could see the sun's rays edging across the sky and where they touched a surface, the upper edge of a roof or the branch of a tree, they glinted and glistened. Frank stood there, slowly turning on the spot in a stillness and radiance as complete as he could imagine. He stopped and held his breath so as not to disturb the spell. Then he heard creaking further along the street and went to investigate. The branches of a large oak were sagging under the weight of a layer of ice and a small branch had succumbed and was lying on the ground, its ice cover still intact. He walked a little further and then went slowly back towards the presbytery. He looked around to take everything in once again before going inside, removing his heavy clothing and heading to the kitchen for breakfast. The wonderland was something he would write about in his next letter home. He started to sketch some sentences as he moved around the kitchen, revelling in the solitude. Then the thought came to him that he had already turned what he had experienced into a memory and it was too soon for that. He set aside what he was doing and went to the front door, determined to go outside and let the scene spread itself through every bit of him until it was indelible. It would become a reference point, a centre of gravity. But when he opened the door his attention was taken by the sight of Father Klein in the middle distance, shuffling his way home. He closed the door quietly and returned to the kitchen.

—

Anja opened the door of the flat. She had on the Thanksgiving dress, now complemented by earrings and a necklace and bright red lipstick. Frank was not sure about the lipstick, but he complimented her on her appearance as he held out the flowers he had brought.

They made their way to the decorated living room. There was a large Christmas tree in the corner, alive with colour and exuding a faint smell of sap.

'The room is beautiful,' Frank said, as Herr Auer and Michael stood up to greet him. 'Like a dream.'

'Poor Frank looks frozen, Anja,' her father said. 'Bring him some mulled wine.'

Frank found himself almost tongue-tied in the presence of the older men, for the first time missing the ease and familiarity of his native language. Herr Auer came to his assistance. 'Our family has a connection to Australia. During the World War my cousin's boy was badly wounded in France. He found himself in an English hospital where some of the nurses were Australian. He said they treated him with great kindness.'

Frank responded that his aunt had been a nurse in France during the Great War, although she never talked much about it. He left unmentioned a conversation in which his aunt had spoken of her aversion when called upon to treat wounded German soldiers.

Cordula appeared in the doorway and summoned everyone to the dining room. She took charge of Frank and showed him where he should sit. He responded by saying that he had seen her at the tram stop in town a few days before. She had been reading a book standing amidst a bustling crowd of people. He said that if he had tried that he would probably have lost his balance and tipped over. Cordula replied that it was not difficult to read standing up, even while walking or on a swaying tram, she had been doing it ever since she was a little girl.

After a short prayer everyone sat down and began to exchange plates and words of thanks through a complicated criss-crossing of arms. As Anja received a full plate from Michael she said: 'You should take Judith with you to Düsseldorf. I don't think she'll wait. I don't know why she chose you in the first place. She should have known where your heart lies.'

Michael did not react to Anja's provocation so she tried a different approach. 'You should come with me to St. Agnes's for midnight Mass. We all should go to St. Agnes's.'

Anja's father pre-empted any response from Michael. 'This family has been attending St. Benedict's for a long time. Your mother is the mainstay of the music. We cannot turn our backs on this parish.'

'Frank, tell Papa what Father Klein said about the Nazis.'

The table quietened and Frank felt compelled to speak. 'He said they are the only ones fighting for Germany and that the Church will soon realise this and withdraw its opposition.'

There was a look of triumph on Anja's face. But Frau Auer said quietly that Lukas's funeral had been at St. Benedict's and they could never leave. And now they should enjoy the food.

For a time everyone ate in near silence. Then Herr Auer put down his knife and fork and addressed his children. 'The Archbishop did not want Lukas to be given a Catholic funeral. He wanted to make an example, to demonstrate the Church's opposition. But Father Klein fought for Lukas, and for us. We are in his debt.'

Anja seemed about to speak but she held back. She looked at her brother and sister in turn but they showed a determined lack of reaction. Eventually the tension subsided and everyone returned to the food.

The conversation gradually picked up. Frank was asked about Australia, and before he could think of where he should start Anja asserted that Christmas could not be properly celebrated in summer. Frank was initially reluctant to mount a defence, but Anja's peremptory tone led him to say that Christmas at home had its own attractions and not everything in Europe was better.

'I'm not saying it is, Frank. But a German Christmas, I'm sure that's the best.'

Dessert arrived in the form of an elaborate cake and the talking converged around this for several minutes. Herr Auer held up a cutting knife and said it was a pity to disturb such a beautiful thing, before plunging the knife expertly into the soft dark mass.

Anja was using a small fork to prise a piece of cake from her plate. As she raised the fork to her mouth she paused. 'What will happen to Father Schapp?'

'Anja, I said we would not talk of that in this house. Why are you determined to spoil this evening for all of us?' Anja made to say something but her father continued. 'We love you without any conditions. You do not need to prove anything to us.'

'I'm not trying to prove anything, Papa. I know you love me.'

Frank's head was bent over his piece of cake. He did not understand the reference to Father Schapp, but he knew better than to say anything. But Anja would not be stopped, and she explained for his benefit.

'There was a report in yesterday's Nazi newspaper about priests abusing young boys. Father Schapp was one of those mentioned. They talked about the Vanguard, the hikes.'

Friedrich Auer slammed the ball of his hand on the table. 'Anja, you will stop this now. This instant.'

Anja wavered. Frank thought she would break into tears, but she recovered herself and announced in an almost steady voice that it was time for the presents.

When the short prayer of thanks for the meal was over chairs were pushed back, but Friedrich Auer remained motionless and the movement stopped. Cordula took her father's hand and then Frank's, prompting a chain of joined hands to form on the table's surface. Frank swallowed awkwardly at the intimacy.

After taking a moment to gather himself Herr Auer spoke. 'The terrible pain of the loss of our son and brother will never leave us, as long as we remain on this earth. But let us look forward to the time when we will be reunited with Lukas in heaven.'

For several seconds no one seemed able or willing to move. Then Marta Auer freed her hands, one from Anja and one from Michael. She stood up and went to her husband and kissed him on the forehead.

When everyone had found their way to the living room Frau Auer sat at the piano and began to play and to sing. The rest of the family soon joined in. Frank's contribution was a silent prayer of thanks for the beauty of the room and the warmth of the people and the fact that he had somehow found his way to this place.

'I want to give Frank his present,' Anja said when there was a break in the music. As she went to the Christmas tree the telephone rang and Frau Auer left the room to answer it.

'Thank you, Anja,' Frank said, blushing slightly as he unwrapped a slim volume of poetry.

'It's about a secret Germany waiting to be resurrected by a new priesthood,' Anja commented, a slightly dismissive note in her voice. 'I thought that sort of thing might appeal to you.'

Before Frank could think of a suitable response Frau Auer called from the doorway that Father Klein wished to speak to him. He put aside his present and followed Frau Auer's directions to the telephone.

The conversation was short, but when Frank returned the living room seemed to have retreated and to be out of reach.

'Frank?'

He looked at the poetry book on the table and then at Anja. 'I'm sorry, I don't have a present for you. I didn't know what to get. Stormy suggested flowers, for the family.'

'Frank?'

'My father telephoned Father Klein. My mother is back in hospital. I will have to go home.' Frank waited and then clarified. 'To Australia.'

Saturday 31 December 1932

A few weeks earlier, when the weather started to turn cold, Anja had dragged Frank along to a shop in the old town. He had not resisted, he knew that with all the ice and snow and sludge to come he needed proper boots. The way Anja had gone about getting the price down, haggling and arguing, was a bit discomfiting, but the thought of the money saved outweighed Frank's embarrassment. He had walked out of the shop fortified in his new boots, the old ones in a box under his arm.

Afterwards Anja had proposed they go to a picture theatre and they had chosen a film from America about a spy during the World War, its theme and Parisian setting promising excitement and love. But after a few minutes Anja had protested that the voices grated and the captions were difficult to read; he could stay if he wanted but she was leaving. He had reluctantly dragged himself away from the adventure and the warm layers of English.

There was another picture theatre nearby showing a German film and they had gone in there. Anja had told the woman in the ticket booth they had gone to the American film by mistake, they had meant all along to come to this German film, she had showed the ticket stubs and the woman had let them in for free. Frank could hardly believe it. Anja had smiled at her victory and led him by the hand into the flickering darkness.

—

Ever since the new boots, whenever he was alone in his room in the presbytery, too tired to read and at a loss for something to do, Frank would take the boots out from under the bed, feel around for the tin of polish and an old piece of cloth and lose himself in a polishing routine that invariably made him think of his father, sitting on the back step of their house surrounded by shoes and boots of varying shapes and sizes, deciding where he should start. On these occasions his dad usually wore an old pair of overalls that flapped around his body like a tent come loose from its moorings. A rusty last used for resoling would be lying on the ground somewhere. Frank had always poked his feet around carefully inside his shoes after his father's resoling work, making sure no tacks were sticking through. His dad had cut their hair too, in the back yard, with an old pair of clippers that every now and then had caught Frank's hair and pulled and caused him to wince and once to swear, which earned him a sharp clip across the ear. He remembered when Ellie, she must have been eleven or twelve, had gone crying to their mother after one of his dad's efforts, fingers pulling at her hair, and after that the two girls had insisted on going to a proper hairdresser in town. But Frank had stayed loyal. The first time his hair had been cut by a real barber was in London at the end of the boat trip from home, and he had not enjoyed the experience. The cutting process itself was smooth, a form of caress unsettling enough in its way. Then there was the large mirror perched in front of him that he had tried to avoid but could not entirely. And when the man held up another mirror so Frank could see the back and sides of his head he had gulped at a view of himself he had never seen before and did not want to see again. 'Yes, that's fine, thank you,' he had said, resisting the temptation to duck away. Thankfully in Siebenkirchen he had found a barber shop with mirrors so dulled by age and smoke that they kept their images largely to themselves.

—

Anja came late on Christmas morning, bringing the book of poems that Frank had left behind. Frau Wolters was in the kitchen, preparing a large portion of potato salad. When she was ready to leave she motioned to Anja to accompany her, but Anja said that Frank should not be left alone. She would stay with him until Father Klein returned from Mass.

When they were alone Anja started to explore, touching things and opening doors and poking her head into rooms until she found what she was looking for. Frank's room was cold and she lay on the bed and covered herself with the old eiderdown. When Frank arrived she held the eiderdown up and said he should come and lie down too. 'Just to keep warm, Frank.'

Frank climbed uncertainly under the covers, his face towards the door. A silence settled over the bed. After a while he felt pressure on his back, Anja was tracing a pattern with her finger. The pressure was not continuous, there were short gaps, and he realised she was writing something. He concentrated hard and thought he could make out individual letters, but he could not form them into words. But whatever it was Anja was writing, he was sure the words were kind and he was thankful for them.

Anja's breathing started to deepen as she sank into sleep. Frank's mind wandered. He was a young boy. His mother had gone on a trip to visit a sick relative and he had missed her terribly. Then one day he had realised he could not picture her face. He had searched his memory but he could not find her face anywhere. And he could not hear her voice. He was betraying her, although he did not mean to. He could still remember his relief when he went with his dad and his sisters to the bus station and he recognised his mum immediately she stepped off the bus.

As he emerged from this memory Frank felt his mouth and his eyes follow a preordained path and he began to sense his face embodying a typical expression of his mother's. She was there, looking out through him, asserting a kinship more vivid and deeper than any image in his imagination. He was glad of this feeling. It steadied him and reminded him of who he was.

He heard knocking on the bedroom door. He must have fallen asleep. He was disoriented, he had no idea where he was, whether it was night or day. He turned his head towards the door. Father Klein was standing there, his hand paused, ready to knock again.

'Father. I must have fallen asleep.' Frank swung his feet onto the floor and stood up facing the priest, brushing at his clothes. 'It was just to keep warm.'

'Fräulein Auer should leave immediately.'

In response to this episode the atmosphere in the presbytery took on a new sourness and the holiday time seemed to Frank as though it would never end. Dull weather, snow replaced by rain, drizzle, little wind, a narrow, enclosed world, not snug but heavy, weighing on him, encompassing him like a snake that wraps itself around you and slowly squeezes the life out of you. And a dismal routine, listening for Father Klein's movements, slipping quietly out of his room to get something to eat when the priest was not in the kitchen, carefully timing his visits to the toilet, Father Klein apparently doing the same, an exhausting minuet.

His father telephoned and the connection was clear. Frank could hear the shaking in his dad's voice, the flatness of the vowels, the warm active night alive and vibrating in the background. He should find out the cost of the boat home and telegraph the details. His dad would send the money straight away.

'Mum has improved, but she has little movement in her right side. She is asking for you.'

After the conversation Frank railed at fate and distance. He wanted to see Anja but worried that Father Klein might have spoken to her father about the bedroom scene, so he stayed away. Then Michael telephoned and said there would be a hike that weekend and Frank was welcome to join. He should have something to eat before he came, there would be no time to stop for lunch, but dinner and breakfast would be provided. He should bring warm clothing and blankets, and a torch.

—

The Vanguarders were gathered around the front of the Auers' apartment building when Frank arrived just after midday. Harald, Theo, August, Jochen, Carl were in one group, Felix and Ollie stood a little to one side. Everyone was in short pants and long socks, but in deference to the cold there were heavy coats and scarves, caps and gloves. Little puffs of condensed air floated around.

The door of the apartment building opened and Michael Auer appeared with a large wicker basket propped against his chest. Anja was helping him, rugged up as if she were going on the hike, tottering under the weight of the basket. Then came Cordula, carrying an assortment of small items, followed by her mother and father.

What followed put Frank in mind of a military parade ground, with the young men lined up in formation and Herr and Frau Auer filing past, shaking hands and exchanging smiles and bestowing every good wish for the hike and for the New Year.

'I feel sure this will be an auspicious year for you all, and for our country.' Friedrich Auer was addressing the company. 'And I feel very confident that with young men like you on our side we will surely win.' He turned and sought out his son and embraced him. Then he took his wife's hand and the two of them went up the steps, turning and giving a small wave before disappearing back into the building.

Cordula followed her parents up the front steps. All eyes were on her as she wished everyone a happy New Year. The chorus-like response left no doubt that her softly spoken words had been heard.

Anja was quickly by Frank's side. 'I don't agree with this. We should spend New Year together.'

She moved closer and lifted up her face and tugged gently on Frank's arm. He bent and kissed her forehead. The sensation on his lips was one of surprising warmth. Then Anja rested herself against him. He felt her bulky coat and her scarf and her fleecy hat and somewhere beneath it all a fluttering heartbeat. They stayed like that, loosely draped together, gently swaying in the still air, until Michael called out that they were leaving. Anja wrapped her arms more tightly around Frank before sending him off with a push.

It was an overcast day with a fluky wind. There was no rain but the air was heavy with moisture, creating a seeping cold. Frank pulled his cap over his ears. He had two jumpers under his overcoat but he could feel the cold against his skin. He flexed his toes inside his boots to reassure himself.

Someone was carrying a long pole with a grey banner. The banner drooped, then fluttered in a minor movement of air and made a light slapping sound. Frank could distinguish the intertwined letters, P and X. The name of Christ, the hope of the world, he could hear his mother saying.

Theo Lindner started to sing. He had a scarf across his face and the sound was muffled and the initial response hardly more than a faint echo. There was no drumming to emphasise the rhythm. But after a while the singing picked up of its own accord and Frank mumbled and hummed along.

Michael gave regular encouragement to everyone to keep up the pace. With darkness setting in early they needed to reach their first stop by four o'clock. Someone from another Vanguard group would meet them and guide them to their destination. The rendezvous point was a wayside shrine.

After several minutes of daydreaming Frank's attention was caught by the distant sound of rhythmic voices. A band of trees and undulations in the landscape hid parts of the view, and the voices had become much louder before the first of the flags and the brown and black clad figures came into clear sight, their swastika armbands adding a splash of colour. The Vanguarders pulled closer together and Theo increased the volume and pace of his singing. The others followed his lead and there was confidence and conviction. But as the brown marchers approached, preceded by what had become a battering ram of sound, the Vanguarders dimmed their voices and slowed their walking, finally coming to a complete stop to allow the long column to cross their path unhindered. Frank's gaze fell on individual marchers and he was struck by their youth, their freshness and apparent fragility. But this impression was fleeting and the young faces were quickly reabsorbed into the trundling, grinding mass.

When the column had passed, the Vanguarders resumed their journey. But now there was no talking or singing, just the sounds of moving feet, each member of the group lost in his thoughts. The countryside seemed to have withdrawn its welcome and replaced it with indifference, if not something more aggressive, mockery or derision, a judgment on the puny resistance that had been offered to the superior force. As Frank thought these thoughts he felt the cold settling heavily on him. He wrapped his coat more tightly around his chest and introduced a skipping element into his forward motion, despite occasional bemused looks from his companions, until his body began to warm and his legs to tire.

They arrived at the shrine a little before four o'clock. They had climbed some way into the hills and there was now only a smattering of trees, bare of all leaves, and little undergrowth. To the left, a steep bank dropped down to a stream, and the sound of the water pushed itself up from below, energetic and mobile. The bank was rocky in parts, with flat, sharp-edged layers of dull-coloured stone, in other parts exposed tree roots. The scene was raw, a piece of rough skin on the point of bleeding. Frank shuddered.

The group congregated around the shrine. It was a simple thing, two wooden poles a few feet apart reaching about five feet above the ground, propping up a small, sharply-angled roof. On a metal frame also affixed to the poles was a picture of the Blessed Virgin, the baby Jesus on one arm, her gaze lowered, her head lightly haloed. The picture featured fruit attached to vines and flowers to stems. The colours would once have been vivid, but time and the elements had leached away the brightness.

Frank saw pale faces among the fruit and the flowers, observing, measuring.

Felix Meyer knelt on the ground and took out his guitar from its case. He removed his gloves, rubbed his hands together, then cupped them in front of his face and blew into them. He picked up the guitar and began to play, isolated notes at first, then a series of arpeggios. He began to recite some words and was joined by a few of the others, asking, despite their youth, for prayers at the hour of their death. Theo added his voice and the words became a song and Frank felt his skin quicken at the bass tones which cast the singers in a light of deep seriousness and holiness. But the music came to an abrupt halt when Felix stopped and apologised, putting his hands in his armpits for warmth. The group dispersed, apart from Jochen, who was left looking fixedly at the shrine.

Michael was with someone Frank had not seen before. 'Everyone, this is Georg. He'll lead us to our destination. On your feet now.'

Felix, standing next to Frank, told him they were going to the old slate mines. His father had once worked there.

'What does your father do now?'

Felix switched the guitar case from his left to his right hand so that it would not be between them as they walked.

'He died in the World War.'

'Oh, I'm sorry, Felix.'

'I hardly knew him. When he left for the war I was only four. He came home once. What I mostly remember is the smell. His uniform had a strong odour, which seemed to have seeped into his body, even his breath.'

Frank said nothing. The two of them were falling behind and they had to concentrate on catching up. They were still climbing and Frank had to fight for each breath.

Eventually the ground levelled out and Frank's breath returned. The trees were now completely gone. Everywhere there were piles of rocks layered and severed at abrupt angles, a deep, moist grey mass catching scraps of low-level cloud which merged with patches of unmelted snow. Derelict pieces of machinery were scattered around, bits of old rope, a hut with a sharply sloping roof and broken windows and a door half off its hinges. There were tracks dug into the side of the hill. Everywhere evidence of human labour, intruding on nature.

Michael and Georg were waiting for the others to catch up. Georg spoke abruptly in tightly wrapped parcels of information and advice. 'The entrance is just up ahead. Use your torches when you have to. Watch where you put your feet, the path can be slippery, there may be ice patches. Near the entrance there's a sharp fall on the right-hand side. Stay well clear of the fence; it's not reliable. We'll go in single file.'

The path narrowed as it headed towards what looked like a sheer rock wall. The low wire fence to the side was in poor condition, broken in parts, offering darkness instead of a faint gleam of metal to the collective torchlight. Frank walked well to the other side of the path. He had no stomach for heights, even those he could not see.

There was no talk as they moved on. Concentration brought sweat to Frank's brow and his armpits. His back ached and his legs felt weak. A voice came from the front saying they were near the entrance and should slow down.

The gate at the mine entrance was dragged aside and the provisions basket passed over the top. Frank's height proved useful in this task although it became a hindrance when they got inside. The passage, a tunnel, was wide enough, but Frank hit his head on something hanging from the roof. The ground was uneven, muddy at the outset with occasional puddles and a set of metal tracks for carts of some sort. Bits of wooden trussing skirted the walls.

Georg's voice pushed through the heavy air. 'Watch your step.'

In the play of light from the torches the tunnel gave no forewarning that it would end. Frank glimpsed a low barrier to his right and kept his distance from it. The passage bent to the left and descended sharply, then widened into a cavern. The general mood lifted.

'There's plenty of room for you all here. But keep to this end. Further along it can get wet. There's sometimes a pond there.'

A few light beams shot up and played across the roof of the mine before the torches were switched off, leaving utter darkness. Then the darkness eased and movement and shapes and limbs began to emerge.

'You can start a fire. The air currents will take care of the smoke.'

For a time no one said anything. A few of the torches flickered on again and there was a general milling around, each deciding with whom he should sit and to which part of the new territory he should lay claim.

Soon a small fire was burning. Frank could see faces reflected in the light and felt a smile form on his face. It must have been the uncanny homeliness of the scene.

'There's a passage behind you, to the left. It leads to a small dunny. There should be some old newspaper still there. If not, I hope you've brought your own.'

'I've got copies of the brown rag. We'll make them a darker brown.' This brought a splash of appreciative laughter for Jochen.

Michael thanked Georg and said they could manage now. Georg disappeared, a shimmer of torch light fading into the gloom, accompanied by the lingering sound of footsteps. No one spoke. Everyone was looking into the fire, sitting or squatting. Frank sensed a change in the general mood, a feeling of being abandoned. Then a voice called out. 'We're very proud of you, Michael. The Vanguard leadership.' Someone started to clap and everyone joined in. The applause echoed around their ears and they pushed further and further until gradually letting it fade. The sombre mood returned.

'What are we doing here, Michael?'

Michael did not directly answer Jochen. Instead he said: 'We have to consider the worst.'

'What's the worst?' August Langscheid asked.

'The Nazis will take over. They will eliminate all opposition.'

'Not the Church.' August's tone was brittle.

'They want here what has happened in Italy. The Church without political influence, the Catholic political party banned. Faith a purely private thing, shut up in itself.'

'And we meet in a cave?' Jochen was forcing a laugh.

'We're not large in numbers but that will not stop them taking the trouble to hunt us down. They will want to claim everyone and everything for themselves. We need to find a way to survive.'

'But they lost votes last time,' August pleaded. 'Everyone said they were finished.'

'They are still the largest party. And their opponents have no common purpose.'

'We will lead the resistance?' Jochen asked, his tone now biting.

'Our meetings will be banned. We will be attacked. We should have our secret places.'

'And one day when we're down here they will come and roll a rock in front of the entrance and leave us to suffocate.'

The prospect depicted by Jochen plunged the group into a period of reflection. The silence was unconvincingly broken by August. 'We'd push the rock away, wouldn't we Michael?'

Michael responded that it was time to eat, his mother had prepared something special for New Year. The contents of the wicker basket were distributed, thick slices of bread with ham and strong mustard, a fruit cake with cherries on top, pieces of dark chocolate, an apple each. When everyone had found a place to sit they took out their thermos flasks.

The light from the fire seemed to retreat into itself, leaving the young men largely in darkness. They exchanged few words while eating.

Frank felt a deep sense of relief as his hunger was stilled, but then the smell of the mine started to seep into his awareness, a mixture of loam and metal, damp and oppressive, and with it came a feeling of hopelessness. Slowly and softly at first, but then extending further inside him and spreading out and merging with the pain in his back and the soreness in his legs, the dull feeling anchored him to the ground. His mind conjured up an image of the Vanguarders cowering deep inside the earth, heads bowed, the exit blocked by an enormous rock, each scooping together a pile of familiar things, a little mound of security, while above ground a deranged mechanical monster, a violent metamorphosis of those hundreds of slender forms and glowing faces from earlier in the day, smashed through the landscape, tearing up every living thing by its roots and flattening the ground in its inexorable path.

'It's creepy here.' Felix was sitting next to Frank. A few of the group had started to move around, casting faint shadows on the walls.

Felix fetched his guitar case, crawling on hands and knees. He went closer to the fire. Harald came and sat with him, holding a mouth organ, and the two of them began to adjust their instruments to one another. They smiled as each sound rebounded off the walls and the roof and died away very slowly. Jochen gave a loud shout and someone answered and this was followed by several other cries, each trying to outdo its predecessor in volume, length or ingenuity.

When the cacophony had played itself out the singing started. Some of the group clapped in time or slapped their hands on their thighs, perhaps as much to keep their hands warm as to keep time.

At one point Frank found himself looking at Jochen, who was sitting very still, making no sound and with a puzzled look on his face, as if singing were a practice he was encountering for the first time. But it might just have been a trick of the light. When Frank looked again Jochen was energetically singing and clapping his hands.

Someone said it was after nine o'clock and Michael announced they should get ready for sleep. They would have to get up very early in the morning to get back to town in time for Mass. He suggested a prayer, and the group knelt.

After the prayer they wished each other every blessing for the coming year, then took it in turns to use the toilet and to wash sparingly in the little pond at the far end of the mine.

Frank settled down to sleep with his coat and boots on, a blanket underneath, one on top, a towel for a pillow. There was a slight murmur of voices and he lifted his head. He could see a number of figures kneeling with heads bowed, dispersed amongst small islands of flickering light, candles which had appeared unannounced and which were now issuing faint threads of smoke he could smell rather than see. He thought he should lift himself onto his knees, clasp his hands, find suitable words to bring the day to an end, to form an intention that would draw the various parts of himself together into something coherent and fine. But he was too tired. He lay his head down and drifted off to sleep.

He was not sure what time it was when he woke. The aftermath of burning candles still hung in the air, a sweet nostalgic smell. The fire had shrunk to a diminutive smoulder, issuing just enough light to temper the profound darkness. He needed a cigarette. He retrieved a pack from the bottom of his rucksack, rolled over and rummaged in his things for the cold hardness of his torch. He crawled towards what he hoped was the tunnel which led outside, avoiding the patches of lighter darkness that were his sleeping fellows. He switched on the torch, holding it close to the ground, and the light skidded across a puddle and banged into a metal surface, an old piece of track. He stood in stages and felt above his head for the roof, grazing his hand on a sharp edge. Stooping slightly, right hand touching the wall and left hand steering the torch, he made his way outside.

He was greeted by a heavy mist and a deep cold. He had not thought to bring his cap or gloves and he cursed quietly to himself. He turned up the collar of his coat. He found somewhere to sit, fumbled for a cigarette with fingers already close to freezing and managed to light it. He dragged in the smoke three or four times and felt a wave of dizziness and then a slow movement of relaxation. He turned off the torch and laid it on the ground. He looked at the burning tip of light and followed it as he moved the cigarette to his lips, then made a circle in the air, then a figure eight. The cigarette was quickly finished. He bent forward and pulled up his knees, resting his forehead against his arms and against the darkness. Slowly the silence took hold of him, bringing his thoughts to a standstill and creating a distance to the cold in his body.

The peace was broken by footsteps. He searched for the torch, switched it on and pointed it towards the sound. Its light tangled with the beam from another torch and he was momentarily blinded. Then he heard a low whisper and responded, with relief. 'It's Frank.'

Jochen was holding a blanket around his shoulders. He knelt down beside Frank.

'I smell a cigarette.'

'I know it's not allowed.'

'Have you got any more?'

Frank took the packet from his coat pocket and held it out. Then he lit a match and Jochen inclined his head towards it.

They sat for a time without speaking, enjoying the collusion. Jochen finished his cigarette and they waited as their eyes adjusted to the loss of the only source of light.

'What do you think of all this?'

Frank felt rather than saw Jochen tilt his head in the direction of the mine.

'What do you mean?'

'Marching and singing and praying and trying to be better than everyone else.'

'I think it's rather fine.' Frank was dissatisfied with the adjective but could think of nothing better.

'I've had enough. I've made up my mind.'

Frank's stomach tightened. Jochen was about to step into the dark, a darkness deeper than the night. The thought made him fear for his comrade, and for himself. But he was also excited. He wanted to know more.

Jochen whispered that they should keep their voices down. 'You know how sound travels at night.'

'Have you told any of the others?'

'You're the first. I've only just told myself.'

'Is it this place?'

Frank was shivering almost constantly. His teeth were chattering. He pulled his coat more tightly around him. 'This time?'

He started to recite: 'The night is a time of otherness, of fear, of excess,' then stopped and wanted to take the words back. He searched for other features of the night that might have brought Jochen to his decision, but was interrupted by his companion's voice.

'The shrine, so much softness. But we need strength, hardness.' Jochen continued after a pause. 'They will come for us with bared teeth, like Michael said. But hiding under the ground, what's the point of that?'

'What will you do?'

'There are groups that will fight.'

'The reds?'

Jochen made a movement which Frank took as affirmation.

'Do you know Max Wolters?' Frank asked. 'He's with the reds.' He wanted to explain about Max, about Frau Wolters, but he held back out of respect for confidences.

'I'm sorry about your mother's illness,' Jochen said, ignoring Frank's question. 'But your father is still alive?'

'Yes,' Frank said eventually, as he fully registered the question.

'In our group Michael and August are the only ones who still have their fathers. All the rest fallen, in the World War. Perhaps that's why we joined the Vanguard. And why some of us are so hard on Michael. We want him to replace our fathers.'

'I think everyone respects Michael.'

'We want to love him. But at the same time we think it's not allowed, so we're confused and discontented.'

Frank thought of his father, of his love for him. Such a simple and obvious thing. He gulped at the thought of where he would be without it.

'Some of the priests are good men. But there's too much softness in them. Father Schapp is soft underneath. Not Father Klein, though. There's a hardness in that man.'

Frank wanted to change the subject. As he waited for a suitable topic to suggest itself a series of distant sounds, of animal origin he was sure, penetrated the air.

'Wolves?' he whispered. He had never heard a wolf's howl so he was guessing. But he was disappointed when Jochen said there were no longer any wolves in Germany; they had all died out or been driven away. Jochen followed up his words with a low-key laugh. Frank thought he understood the laugh and tried to return it, but then felt awkward and presumptuous. He took out a cigarette, lit it and held the glowing end near his watch. Midnight. 'Happy New Year,' he said, reaching out to touch Jochen.

III

The Room : January – February 1933

Monday 9 & Saturday 14 January 1933

Bill had pushed his bed hard against the wall and the dresser was shoved into the corner at the foot of the bed, a small desk wedged between the two. Frank had bought a second-hand mattress and Jak, Bill and Stormy had helped to carry it through the freezing streets and manoeuvre it up the stairs. They had squeezed it in at right angles to Bill's bed, the only way you could get the door open with the mattress down. Bill said that it would not be for long. Once a bigger room was available they would move, provided it was not too expensive.

'Are you sure about this, Frank?' Bill had asked him beforehand.

They had been in the mensa, just the two of them, the first day after the holiday. They were speaking German, in accordance with an undeclared pact. Frank was talking about his mother's illness, something that in his mind was not compatible with the energetic woman he knew, and he found himself saying he might put off going home and an intention to stay formed as he spoke. It would be such a waste if he could not finish the semester, he said. He was finally starting to feel at home in the language, it was seeping deeper and deeper into him, becoming part of him, expanding him. If he left now he might never be able to return.

'But I won't stay at Father Klein's,' he added. 'I feel trapped there.'

Bill said that Frank should think carefully about his decision to delay his return home. This country and its language could cast a spell, promise a special seriousness, a greater depth of experience, but this was probably an illusion.

'But you're still here, Bill. Living on a shoestring.'

Bill's face broke into a smile of acknowledgement. 'Come too far,' the two of them said, almost simultaneously. Frank felt a momentary light-heartedness, but Bill brought him back to earth. 'But don't they need you back home?'

To avoid answering Frank asked a question of his own. 'Do you think Jak is right? There will be a...cataclysm?'

Bill's response seemed to come of its own accord. 'Many people here think they have nothing to lose. And who can blame them.'

Frank looked around. The normality of the mensa, its talk and laughter and togetherness, seemed to belie Bill's words. He tried briefly to imagine what it would be like to have nothing to lose, but quickly gave up. There were too many things binding him to his life.

A satchel thudded onto the table and Frank looked up to see Anja. 'I'm moving in with Bill,' he said to her.

Anja replied that she knew all along that would happen.

—

Bill had been out all afternoon, giving English lessons for a pittance. As soon as he opened the door of the room he told Frank they needed to go.

'It's raining,' he added. 'Should be snowing, this time of year. Would be back home.'

Bill picked up some tins of food and put them into a bag. 'You should bring a knife and fork, and a cup.' He pointed to a loaf of bread. 'And the bread.'

Outside all traces of daylight were gone. The rain was steady and soaking. Frank set off in pursuit of Bill, but after a few steps he felt himself kick something on the pavement. The thing gave a little against his foot then scampered away, and Frank recoiled in disgust.

The street lights were weak, a faint wash through the rain. Frank felt himself sweating under his coat. A door was flung open directly in front of him and light and sound spilled out, loud voices and laughter. A large figure loomed up and forced its way past him. Frank lost control of the loaf of bread and it fell to the ground. More jostling figures emerged. Frank tried to push through them, stretching out a hand for the dropped loaf. He could smell cigarette smoke and stale beer, and bile rose in his throat. He looked up and saw Bill appear out of the darkness, striding towards him.

'Come on, Frank.'

'Where are we going?' He was hunching over to protect the recovered bread from the rain.

They turned in at a house which was distinguished from its neighbours by a pole jutting from the front and a flag sagging in the rain.

A plaque glinted on the wall, but Frank did not bother to read it. Bill pushed open the heavy front door and motioned him through. 'They lock the door at six on weekends. We're just in time.'

It was quiet inside, and dark. Bill felt for a switch on the wall and a dim light came on. He led the way along a corridor, opened a door on the right and turned on another switch. The light showed they were in a kitchen.

'What is this place?'

'Frat house.' Bill said this in English and Frank was taken by surprise.

Bill pointed to a white box-like object sitting on four squat legs with a circular structure on top, like the conning tower of a submarine.

'Ice box,' Bill said, reverting to German. 'I'm not supposed to use it. But occasionally I slip something in.'

Bill opened a cupboard above a sink with two sturdy-looking taps. 'I keep my plates and things here. There's room enough for yours as well.'

'What did you say this place was?' Frank could see a patch of mould spreading up the wall under the sink. He thought he could smell damp and looked around for further signs of decay, but found none.

'Frat house. You know, fraternity?' Frank looked blank. 'Student society. We have them at home, but not like here. Here they go way back. Quaint uniforms and duelling. But this one is supposed to be different. No duelling, moderate drinking.' Bill was spooning baked beans into a pan which he placed on the stove, a modest thing sitting in the far corner. 'Why don't you cut some bread, make toast. I'll boil the water. We can have something hot to drink. I've got cocoa.'

As the kettle started to make sounds of stress Bill opened a flat can which he put on the table. He set down a jar of jam beside it. Frank gave him a questioning look.

'I've eaten so many damned sardines since I've been in this country that I just can't take the taste any more. But they're cheap and filling, so I spread marmalade over them. Helps me get them down.'

'So you eat here?' Frank said, to mask a feeling of nausea.

'I know one of the head guys. He squared it away with the others. I get to use the kitchen, store stuff, come in early before the others. It's a lifesaver on weekends and holidays, when the mensa's closed.

But we shouldn't dawdle. The others usually start to drift in around seven. We need to be gone by then.'

Despite the stove being in use the air was cold. Frank saw a heater attached to one of the walls but did not ask about turning it on. The baked beans began to do him good, and the hot drink. Sitting there with Bill he felt like he was part of a conspiracy that could not fail.

'It's cosy here,' he said, trying to suppress a shiver.

'Hunkered down,' Bill replied. 'Waiting for the storm to blow over.'

Frank thought of the slate mine and the feeling of well-being dissipated. He shivered again and looked up at the ceiling. 'Quiet though. How many people live here?'

'A dozen or so, maybe more. Don't see them. Don't want to see them.'

'Why not?'

'I take each person on his merits, not whether he belongs to this club or that society. I don't hold with that.'

Frank thought of the Vanguard, and he wondered what would happen now Michael was gone. He was not sure there was anyone who could replace Michael. Perhaps others would follow Jochen's example and the group would unravel.

'I suppose so,' he said vaguely.

The pair sat in silence for several minutes, finishing their meal. Frank observed Bill's ritual with the sardines and the jam. He wondered if it was an American practice, not just Bill's idiosyncrasy, but did not want to ask.

The door opened and a heavy-set young man of around their own age came in. Bill glanced at his watch, shot to his feet and started clearing things from the table. Frank stood up as well.

'Who's this, Bill?'

'Frank. He's moved in with me. Frank, this is Ulf.'

The newcomer seemed to exude overweening confidence and to flow into all parts of the room, appropriating it.

'You should have asked me, Bill.'

'We'll be gone. A couple of minutes.'

'I'm not sure. The others are unhappy. Someone found the toilet in a mess. A turd in the bowl. Seems to think it was you. And there was something of yours in the ice box.'

'Do my turds smell different?'

Ulf scrunched up his face. 'There's been a threat to tell the governors about our arrangement. If that happened it would go badly for me.' Ulf hesitated, as if he were exploring the shape that things going badly might take. 'You'll have to make other arrangements.'

'Shit.'

The English curse word in Bill's mouth startled Frank. He juggled the cup he was holding.

'We've hanging on in this damn country by the skin of our teeth.' Bill was standing still and staring at Ulf. 'You should be grateful.'

'Grateful?'

'Germany is heading for the wall. Seems the only ones with any grip are the foreigners. If you get rid of us you'll be left to yourselves and everything will go to hell.'

Ulf assumed a pose of authority. 'Germany is in its current position because of the unfair conditions imposed on it at the end of the World War. Your country thinks only of itself. Now Germany has to think of itself. And act for itself. It won't be long now.'

Bill suddenly looked exhausted. 'Can I leave my things here in the meantime?'

'One more week. But no longer.'

Tuesday 31 January 1933

Anja was in tears. She was standing next to Stormy Weather, who looked lost, his head moving from side to side like a stricken bird. One hand was reaching in Anja's direction but it hesitated to touch her, as if rebuffed by a physical force. Jak was pawing the floor, waiting for an opening to charge through.

Frank and Bill arrived together, talking animatedly as they came up the stairs, two steps at a time. They had been to inspect a new room, bigger and with its own cooking facilities. It was much more expensive, but Frank would cover the additional cost. It would have to come from the ticket money, but that was a problem for later.

The mensa was unusually still. The clinking of plates and cups and knives and forks, the clatter of trays on tables, all this was muted, and the hum of voices was almost oppressive in its restraint.

'Jesus!' As soon as he had said the word Frank could hear Margie's voice, her delight in the prospect unmistakable. 'Daddy will wash your mouth out with soap.'

A glance at the table was enough. Bobby O'Donnell was sitting there, with Charles Smith and Ray Wright. Ernst Tüchnow was there too, and Arnie Wriedt and a bevy of other figures in brown shirts, some of them standing, all of them looking relaxed and menacing at the same time. A bright red flag with a white circle and a black swastika covered the pale wood of the table. And carefully arranged on top, like holy objects on an altar, were elaborately framed photographs of the Nazi leaders.

Bobby stood up. He was wearing a version of the table covering on his right arm. He raised the arm crisply in a Hitler salute and held it there. His tone was serious.

'In the light of yesterday's elevation of Adolf Hitler to Reichschancellor, we consider it only right that the new order be reflected in this university. In our own small way we are bearing witness to the dawn of a new Germany, to the rebirth of a great nation. Heil Hitler.'

The other members of the table's contingent sprang to their feet and, together with those already standing, replicated Bobby's salute and repeated his incantation.

'You've made your point,' Bill said, stepping forward. 'Now we'd like our table back.'

'I don't think you quite understand. Or you are being deliberately obtuse. This is our table now.' Bobby spread his arms in an encompassing gesture. 'Our country.'

'Your country?'

Somewhere someone started to sing. Frank thought he recognised the tune, a marching song not so different from those the Vanguarders sang on their hikes. Soon there were supporting voices from the table and from elsewhere across the room. The sound reverberated and deepened. And in the midst of it all Bobby O'Donnell's face bright with belonging, brimming with belief. For a moment Frank found himself unable to begrudge Bobby his happiness. This time he felt sure it was not just for show.

As the singing reached a crescendo Bill Parker leant forward and took one end of the flag in both his hands and jerked his arms back. The photographs in their frames seemed for a moment to hang in mid air, then they toppled and clattered onto the floor, their glass panels splintering. The singing ceased, as if the air sustaining it had been cut off. Bill stood there with the flag in his hands. He used one corner to wipe something off his coat, then dropped it on the floor and kicked it away.

Arnie Wriedt was on his feet, a number of the others too. They approached Bill, who stood his ground. One gave a sharp push, causing Bill to stumble backwards and almost lose his feet.

'Fuckin' leave him alone!'

In response to Jak's outburst one of the brownshirts went purposively up to him and kneed him hard in the groin. 'Ahhrg, shit.' Jak doubled over and vomited. A pair of hands grabbed him and propelled him downwards and as his body hit the floor it sent some of the vomit squirting across the tiles. There was more pushing and shoving and Bill tripped and fell. He put his hands around his head for protection as one of the brownshirts kicked at him. At the edge of the fracas Anja started to swing her satchel, but it was torn from her hands and thrown on the ground and stamped on.

A rush of rage hit Frank. He wanted to kick each of the aggressors and send them writhing to the floor in agony, Bobby O'Donnell included. He would stamp on Bobby's face, squash the smirk, enjoy the sound of cracking cheek-bones.

But this fantasy was interrupted by a heavy blow to his head. He tried to tell them to leave Bill alone, it was not a fair fight, but he had no voice. He was back home, there had been a card game and by some fluke he had won a hand. His mum had been in bed and he had rushed to her room to tell her of his triumph but had tripped and hit his head. When he had got himself back on his feet and tried to speak the words had refused to leave his mouth. He had stood there high and dry, mind and mouth moving to no avail, arms flapping and head bobbing, just like now.

Arnie Wriedt picked up a chair and slammed it into Bill's head. One of the legs wobbled. Again the chair crashed into Bill, one leg now hanging loose. Anja let out a piercing shriek. Bobby called out that it was enough and Ernst stood up and held out a hand to signal stop. But the chair smashed into Bill one more time, then another. Then Arnie Wriedt let the pieces of wood drop to the floor.

Ernst asked in a raised voice whether there were any medical students there and a thin youth came forward tentatively. He knelt beside Bill and started to examine him.

'What in heaven's name is going on?' An officious looking man in a suit was rushing into the refectory. One of the servery women was with him.

'It is over now, sir,' Ernst said, assuming command. 'This man, a foreigner, was guilty of an act of gross desecration. My friends felt compelled to stand up for the honour of Germany.'

'There might be internal bleeding. Someone should telephone for an ambulance.' The medical student was growing into his role. The suited man said there was a telephone in his office. He gestured to the woman from the servery, who hurried towards the exit.

'Nothing like this, ever before. In all the years.' The man was turning this way and that. He called after the woman. 'The police as well. Ambulance and police.' Then he addressed the room, confident in his authority. 'No one is to leave. The police will want to speak to everyone. If you miss your lectures I'm sorry. But no one is to leave.' He walked to the servery and spoke to the women there, two of whom went and took up positions at the refectory entrance.

Bobby O'Donnell and Ernst Tüchnow exchanged looks. Then Bobby nodded to Charles Smith and Ray Wright and they pushed back their chairs and stood up. Ernst moved around the table, bent and picked up the crumpled flag, folded it neatly and held it in two hands in front of his chest. He then started to walk towards the exit. Like a priest walking down the aisle after Mass, Frank thought. And he watched as Bobby followed Ernst, their respective formations falling into line behind them.

'What do you think you're doing?' The incredulity of the man in the suit raised the pitch of his voice. 'I said no one is to leave.' He moved after the retreating figures.

Ernst and Bobby and the others continued their procession. The man in the suit made to grab an arm but at the last instant his hand fell back to his side. The mensa was quiet.

One of the women at the entrance stepped forward. Her apron had once been white, but washing had dulled it to a weak grey. She had a green cloth tied over her hair. She was a hefty figure, broad and squat, and she blocked most of the exit.

When Ernst reached the woman he took the flag he was carrying and solemnly handed it to her. She accepted the offering dutifully and stepped aside to allow the parade to continue its progress. Frank could hear their footsteps as they descended the stairs, steady and unhurried. He looked across at Bill, still lying motionless under the attentions of the medical student, then looked up and saw two ambulance men hurrying into the room. 'Over here,' he called out, hardly realising that his voice had returned.

Thursday 16 – Friday 17 February 1933

The streets of Düsseldorf were dark and freezing and Michael walked briskly to keep warm. His mind was racing too, replaying the call to arms for the forthcoming election that was to appear in the Catholic newspapers the next day.

In the light of a doorway he caught sight of a congregation of brownshirts, coaxing more than harassing, drawing attention to a rally that was about to begin. He started to skirt around them but then turned and followed the invitation inside, out of curiosity. He half expected to be identified immediately as a foreign body and humiliated and expelled, but instead he was welcomed into a warm atmosphere of youth, belief and commitment which attracted him even as the symbols and the slogans repulsed him. His initial resistance to the exuberance was interrupted by glimpses of Lukas. Suddenly, whichever way he turned, he could see his brother's silhouette, his posture, his face. He started to perspire heavily and pushed his way to the exit. Outside he was jeered by a group of reds, who had gathered for battle. The thought came that he should explain himself to them, but the absurdity of this stopped him in his tracks. He hurried back to his room.

It was still dark when he left for work early the next morning, but as he approached the Vanguard headquarters he could see Father Karlheinz Weidemeier pacing up and down at the front of the building, impatiently glancing at his watch. The two men hardly spoke as they entered the building. They settled in Michael's office, a cubicle of glass in one corner of a large room, then took their time to examine the day's Catholic newspapers. Father Weidemeier broke the silence. 'The statement is powerful. It will not go unheard. And I've heard praise for your role from several quarters.'

Michael did not try to hide his satisfaction at finally seeing the statement in print. The endless meetings and telephone calls of the preceding weeks, the placating, reconciling and reformulating, were now made worthwhile by this united call from the country's Catholic lay organisations to reject the overtures of the National Socialists.

'I particularly like the appeal to the spirit of the great papal encyclicals,' Father Weidemeier continued. 'I fear many of our people have never read these wonderful texts, or have not understood them, or have forgotten them.' The priest looked again at the newspaper he was holding. 'And I see your influence in the reference to sins against youth. The incitement to hatred and revenge, seeds of devastation.'

'The words "sin" and "devastation" were the subject of debate among us. But they are nothing but the truth.'

'Yet so many of our youth see salvation where we see destruction. Don't you wonder about this, Michael?'

'Special interests and divisions of class and station all done away with, replaced by self-sacrifice in a common cause. Many young people think this will purify them. They see social and personal redemption in one doctrine.' As he spoke Michael could feel the pull of the sentiments he was describing. He could see Lukas, but recoiled from offering his brother as an example.

'But it is all filled with so much self-deception,' the priest replied.

'Yes.'

Michael turned his head and looked out through the glass partition. The other Vanguarders were starting to arrive, they were talking among themselves, some standing and reading over the shoulders of those sitting, their intensity and togetherness reminding Michael of the heady atmosphere that had greeted him several months earlier when he had walked into this place, not knowing what to expect.

—

On that Saturday the previous November Michael had been the last of the Vanguard leaders from all over the country to arrive, and when he had entered the room the others had been in animated discussion, constantly swivelling on their chairs, throwing their hands about, laughing and interrupting each other. The theme had been the Nazi setback in the election, the beginning of the end for them, so everyone was saying.

When they had turned to the business of the meeting Peer Scharenberg had explained, at first tentatively but then with increasing conviction and pride, that he and Simone had decided to marry. The wedding would be in January, a winter wedding but he hoped they would all come. The two of them had long been thinking about this step and now was the right time. But it meant he would have to relinquish his position as national head of the Vanguard. The meeting was to choose his successor.

'Congratulations, Peer, my very best wishes to you and Simone.' With a handshake as accompaniment this was all that each of them had been able to offer.

An inconclusive discussion about procedures for choosing Peer's replacement had followed, then Father Weidemeier had pronounced Michael the one best suited to the task. The priest had listed the decisive character traits – resourcefulness, imagination and initiative. Michael had been unsure whether he recognised himself in these descriptions, but his doubts had been allayed when the others had applauded Father Weidemeier's assessment.

Later there had been talk of politics. Father Weidemeier had suggested that the Vanguard could help to keep the Catholic Party on a sensible course at a time when it was in danger of fatal compromises. Peer's response, while remaining within the boundaries of suitable deference, had dismissed the pettiness and partisanship of politics and extolled the universality of the Church. There was enthusiastic support for this point of view from the others. All the different parties scrabbling for pieces of the country. Young people would not stand for it any longer, they wanted unity.

Michael remained on the periphery of this debate, his thoughts occupied by Judith. They had also been talking, tentatively and privately, about a winter wedding, and he could see and hear her disappointment. But he knew that he could not forego the opportunity he had been given. In the event Judith had reacted with a mixture of grudging acceptance and pride that had left him humbled and grateful and able to concentrate fully on what was to come.

—

'The bishops' election statement will appear in the coming days,' Father Weidemeier went on. 'You will need to read between the lines, but our people are well skilled at that.'

'The bishops must be unambiguous,' Michael asserted. 'This is no time for subtlety.'

'If the Church were unified we could mount an offensive that would sweep the godless and the idolaters from the face of the earth.' Father Weidemeier seemed taken aback by the force of his own words. He tone became subdued. 'But how many of our German Catholics have shown themselves willing to make accommodations with the Hitler party. They long for someone to lead them out of the wilderness.'

Michael did not respond. He seemed distracted by a burst of laughter which spilled in from the main office.

'And then there is Rome,' the priest continued. 'It sees Bolshevism as the main threat. And I fear our German bishops lack the depth of conviction to argue the point.'

'The bishops must convince Rome,' Michael demanded.

Father Weidemeier raised his hands in a gesture of resignation. He got to his feet. 'Just two weeks to the election and so many cities still to visit. I only hope my voice is up to the task.'

'Be careful, Father. They will step up their attacks on the meetings. They will stop at nothing.'

The two men shook hands. 'Keep the Vanguard alive, Michael. Keep the love of Christ burning in the hearts of these wonderful young men. This love will prevail. In the end.'

Saturday 25 – Tuesday 28 February 1933

A nun was the instructor. She was overweight but light on her feet, with her habit hitched up somehow to make things easier. She took one of the girls as a partner. As the piano started Frank stole a look in its direction. The nun interrupted. 'Thank you, Mrs Boylan, could we just take that again from the beginning.' A few of the girls were giggling, some of the boys smirking. 'Get those stupid grins off your faces. Let's see how you perform. Take your partners.' The nun grabbed the arm of one of the boys and placed it firmly on his partner's shoulder, the other at the girl's waist. 'Hold her firmly, she won't break.'

Frank remembered this scene as he reached his arms towards the swirl of colour that was Anja, arrayed in a purple waistcoat and yellow blouse and blue and red polka dot pants. He tried to get the pressure right. But he had drunk too much punch and it had not settled in his stomach. And the press of people was almost overwhelming, the music loud and brassy and adamant. Frank struggled with his discomfort, but the touch of Anja's body gradually soothed him and he found himself responding ever more deeply to her responses.

Hours later they came across Felix, also done up in gaudy carnival fashion but looking incomplete without his guitar. Felix said there was a rumour there would be a visit, rabble-rousers, they should be careful. But Anja discounted this and dismissed Felix. She told him Cordie was not there, it was too frivolous for her, and anyway she was not interested in him. He should forget her and find someone else. Frank tried to soften the impact of the words on Felix, but then wondered whether they were really meant for him.

When Frank and Anja left at midnight they did not have to wait to collect their things from the cloakroom. No one else was leaving. The hall was overflowing with the revellers' determination to extract as much pleasure from the night as possible.

Outside, several clusters of young men were pushing and shoving, laughing and smoking. Anja hurried Frank towards a car parked by the kerb. Someone was bending beside the door, talking to the driver through a slightly opened window. The figure did not straighten until they were quite close. Then it raised an arm in a Hitler greeting, turned and took a few steps away. Anja tensed and swore.

'We've been warned the reds might try something tonight,' Ernst Tüchnow called out. 'I've been telling Herr Auer to be on his guard.'

Anja freed herself from Frank. She picked up a stone and threw it in one motion. It missed its target but hit the car.

'That was a stupid thing to do,' Friedrich Auer scolded when Frank and Anja had got themselves inside the car. 'And I won't have that language.'

'You didn't recognise him, Papa?'

'They all look the same to me.'

Friedrich Auer started the motor and edged the car forward, crawling along, not venturing far from the kerb, cowering almost.

'Just trying to humiliate you,' Anja said after a while.

'They cannot humiliate me if I refuse to be humiliated.'

As the car came to a stop outside Frank's building he started the difficult process of extracting himself from the back seat. Anja's father spoke to him as he watched his progress in the rear vision mirror. 'Tonight was against my better judgment. But the carnival ball is one of our traditions. We will not let them take everything from us.'

—

Bill and Frank had already paid the first month's rent for the new room. Stormy and Jak had again helped with the move, with Anja directing where the various pieces of furniture should go. Afterwards they had sat together and compared notes from their interviews with the police. They knew that Ernst Tüchnow and Bobby O'Donnell had also been interviewed, but there had been no arrests. Arnie Wriedt had disappeared, Jak said.

They did not return to the table in the mensa. Anja and Frank spent their lunch-times at the hospital with Bill, who had still not regained consciousness, while Stormy and Jak went to the small mensa near the river. Jak would come to the hospital later in the afternoon and Stormy in the evening. This was the pattern they had fallen into.

If Anja and Frank did not have lectures in the afternoon they would go to Frank's room, doing their best to slip in unseen. Once inside they would give vent to their restlessness. They would sit, stand up and walk around, pick things up and put them down, glance at Bill's bed, made up and neat, sit down and light a cigarette.

On a whim Frank had bought a radio, a box-like thing in hard black bakelite, an extravagance, the eighty marks coming from his money for the trip home, now an indefinite, shapeless prospect. He would turn the radio on and he and Anja would lie on his bed, fully clothed. They would nestle against each other, hardly speaking, dozing to the tones of scratchy music. Often when Frank awoke he would take several seconds to find his bearings. In these brief, unmoored moments the music was just sound waves beating against his head, and he felt helpless and panicky. He was relieved when his mind came back to itself, even if the return was accompanied by a jolt of painful emotion at the thought of Bill.

Anja would leave in the late afternoon and Frank would prepare his dinner in the tiny kitchen, enjoying the practicality of the tasks. Often after eating he would venture outside and walk through the narrow alleyways to the river. He liked the flowing water's hushed silence, the dark accent it gave to the approaching night. But after walking along the river bank for a few hundred yards he would invariably start to lose confidence, the sight of homeless men and women scattered under bridges would unsettle him, and he would hurry back to the room, keeping his head lowered as groups spilled out of pubs or flats. Sometimes the voices were a low murmur and there was soft laughter that offered a moment of vicarious companionship. At other times the sounds were harsh and hostile and they caused Frank to shrink inside his clothes and increase his speed.

Later he would do his assignments and read for his classes. The heating was sparse and he would keep his overcoat on, his gloves too when he was not writing. But despite the cold he was cosy with the lamplight and his books and the German words, increasingly intimate and promising. He would read aloud and enjoy the company of his own voice. And every now and again he would try a different route to a book's promise, burying his nose in its pages and sniffing the fusty smell of ink and old paper, letting his fingertips play with the different textures, searching for something elemental behind the words. The radio would be on softly in the background and sometimes he would stop to listen to a melody that pleased him. He would then return to his book, invariably and mysteriously to the exact place where he had left off. When he tired he would occasionally turn the dial to find the spoken word, fighting his fatigue and listening closely to follow what was being said. Mostly the voices were calm and they would put him at ease. But sometimes the tone was shrill, the words threatening and menacing in advance of their meaning. He would listen as if spellbound, then click off the machine and try to expel the hostile impact from his mind and body.

He had taken to saying his prayers in German. Some of the prayers he had learned by heart, for the others he devised an impromptu translation. He often lost himself in this work. It saved him from wondering whether he was just talking to himself.

—

The walk to the hospital was different, not just from yesterday, a Sunday, when the almost deserted streets exaggerated the sound of his steps, but from every other day. There was a mass of people milling around, in costumes if anything more exorbitant than those at the ball. And there was a parade, floats of all sorts clattering past.

Frank stopped to look. He thought he recognised the figures on one of the floats. The little man with one small shoe and one large boot was the propaganda minister, he was everywhere in the newspapers. And the fat one in the extravagant uniform, he had seen that figure and that face many times. The leader was there too. He kept trying to stand on his hands but he could not bring it off, he kept crashing down, looking around sheepishly to see if anyone had witnessed his ineptitude. The little man was trying to stop him from falling but the fat one was strolling around with his head in a cloud of cigar smoke and he kept bumping into the other two. People in the crowd were pointing and laughing, shouting advice, egging each other on to ever more disrespectful suggestions. Frank was laughing too, for the first time in a long time, so it seemed to him. He looked around to see if he was drawing attention to himself but saw nothing but encouragement. The mood was light and unforced, not tense and shrill like at the ball. He tried to think of something to shout out but nothing came and then he thought that anyway he did not have the right. As the float moved on Hitler managed to stand on his hands for a few seconds, supported by the other two. The crowd booed and Frank joined in.

Anja was waiting for him outside the hospital, impatiently walking up and down. He apologised for being late and then described the scene on the float and the crowd's reaction, taking different approaches to try to capture the pure jubilation of it. But Anja was unimpressed. She took his arm and hurried him inside.

The burly man was sitting next to the bed. Frank wondered what he must be thinking. He never said anything about his feelings for his son. When he spoke it was all about the fact that he did not understand what had possessed Bill to come here. And surely there must be a doctor or a nurse who spoke English? But these impatient words were belied by the man's demeanour, which was that of a large figure seeking to occupy only as much space as was necessary.

Frank had acted as interpreter, but the information he could relay was of little comfort. The doctors had only been able to say that they did not know how long Bill would be in a coma or what state he would be in if he ever woke up.

They found some chairs and sat down as quietly as they could. Bill's father did not look up. Some minutes passed, then a nurse came and stood behind him. She seemed about to speak but then changed her mind and moved away.

'What did she want?' Mr. Parker asked.

'I don't know, sir.'

The nurse returned, wheeling a folding screen which she placed between Mr. Parker and the neighbouring bed. She retraced her steps without speaking.

'He's gone, you know,' Bill's father said.

Frank felt Anja's gaze on him. He bowed his head. Anja started to cry and he put his arm around her. His own tears came, slowly at first then in convulsive gulps. The legs of his chair gave an eerie screech as they scraped on the floor.

Mr. Parker looked up and Anja said that he must hate Germany. Frank translated, not sure if he should, unsure of his voice.

The man included Anja in his gaze as he replied. 'I'm trying to keep my heart free from hate. Bill's gone to God. I don't understand the reasons, but there is a lot in this world I don't understand.' Frank whispered the meaning to Anja, his eyes on Bill's father. 'Perhaps if you could leave me now? I would like to just sit here alone with my boy. I appreciate you coming, I thank you for it. And I thank you for your friendship with Bill.'

Frank stood up. He touched Anja, who also stood. They were briefly motionless, then Anja bent forward and placed her lips on Bill's forehead. She straightened herself, moved around the bed to where Mr. Parker was sitting and stood in front of him. 'Wir hatten Bill lieb,' she said quietly. Frank translated. 'We all loved Bill.'

—

When they got to the room they lay down on the bed with their coats and scarves still on. Frank did not bother to turn on the radio. He could sense Anja shaking beside him and he took hold of her hand. He thought to himself that he could not justify the new room now, with Bill gone.

There was a sharp knocking. Frank eased himself free from Anja and went to the door.

'Yes, Frau Brekker?'

The landlady handed him some washing, sheets and towels and pillow cases. He expressed his thanks, relieved as always that this transaction passed without any sideways looks suggesting recriminations or shared secrets. Frau Brekker asked if the other young man was still in the hospital and Frank said he was. He made to close the door but Frau Brekker put up a restraining hand. 'Did I see a young woman?'

'We are having our lunch.'

'I've seen her before, haven't I?' The woman dropped her head to get a better view inside the room, but Frank stretched out an arm to the door jamb to block her line of sight. 'This is a respectable house. I won't have anything like that.'

When Frank returned to the bed Anja was shivering. 'Can't you turn up the heating?' It was a question Anja regularly asked and he did not bother to answer.

When he lay down again Anja pressed her body against his. At first he thought it was just for warmth, but then he felt her hand press against his crotch. 'Anja, don't.' He put his hands on her arms and exerted a gentle pressure, but she shrugged herself free. She fumbled with the fly of his pants, cold hands on the buttons, finally getting them open. Frank gave up any resistance. 'Please Frank.'

She pressed her forehead into his chest. 'Touch me.' He traced the outline of her body with his hand. Then he tried to find her mouth to kiss, he realised he had not yet kissed her on the mouth, the proper order of things should be followed. But her face was buried somewhere beneath him, and he kissed the top of her head instead.

Again there was a knock on the door. Frank eased himself away, half apologetically, and Anja put her fingers to her lips. Then a raised voice asked if the young woman was gone.

Frank composed himself. 'She's gone, Frau Brekker.' He held his breath until he heard the shuffling sound of retreating footsteps. He caught Anja's eyes and they both smiled. But as they settled back in the bed and found each other's hands the smiles gave way to tears.

—

As they prepared something to eat Anja said in a distant voice that she wanted to stay the night. Frank did not try to argue. There was still plenty of time before the last tram, and he hoped she would come to her senses. But time passed, darkness set in and Anja gave no sign of changing her mind. Then she put on her coat and gloves and made for the door, saying she would find a telephone to speak to her father. Frank relented and went with her.

The air was sharp and a light wind played against their faces. There were few people about and the occasional footfalls reverberated into the night. Then out of nowhere two figures appeared, pursuing them. Anja gave a start, but Frank reassured her. They were just shadows, cast by a fountain with an innocently embracing boy and girl mounted on top.

The post office was near the river and Albertstraße was the shortest route. They walked quickly, pressed together. Before long they crossed over and turned into a side street. About thirty yards ahead two trucks were parked. Heavy boots were clanging on the pavement and fists and rifle butts were banging on the door of an apartment building. A window pane shattered, a door of one of the trucks slammed, an engine started and then fell silent. As they watched several figures were dragged onto the pavement and kicked savagely. Frank could feel the blows in his own body and he started to groan in sympathy. One of the brownshirts yelled something in his and Anja's direction. It was unintelligible, but the threat it contained was unmistakable.

They retreated to Albertstraße and stood catching their breath. Then a truck appeared out of nowhere and lumbered past them towards the river. The commotion of its movement fully registered in Frank's mind only after it was well past, and the jeers and shouts of its exuberant crew seemed to take an eternity to dissipate. Frank stood there as if mesmerised, and Anja grabbed at him. 'They're in a killing mood. We have to hurry.'

Anja took the lead, her limp more pronounced than usual. She put Frank in mind of a small ship in choppy seas, tossing and listing and summoning all its strength to reach the safety of harbour.

—

They walked to the tram stop early the next morning through throngs of brownshirts, some casting challenging eyes, seemingly to provoke a reaction that would justify them in lashing out, others looking exhausted, as if they had not slept for days. The atmosphere was saturated with the indecipherable shouts of newsboys.

Frank himself had hardly slept. There had been a desperate knocking in the middle of the night and he had opened the door to Jak, shouting under his breath that the club had been raided, the storm troopers had come in a frenzy, there had been casualties on both sides.

'They know where we live. And Jak thought of you.' Frank recognised the steady voice of Max Wolters, who was standing in the dark next to Jak.

Once they were in the room there had been a collective listening to the world outside, to the creaking of the building, to occasional footfalls in the corridor, to engine noises and human voices from the street. Frank had related in whispers his and Anja's experience near the post office and asked whether the events might be related, but there had been no clear answer. Anja had made something hot to drink and she and Jak had exchanged some desultory words about Bill. Then the room had settled down for what remained of the night, Anja and Jak occupying the two beds, Frank and Max on the floor. The last thing Frank remembered before finally falling asleep was an incongruous feeling of satisfaction that he could return Max's favour, from what now seemed like a lifetime ago.

—

Anja almost missed her tram. They were not paying attention, they were leaning against each other with their heads down, a number of trams were coming and going and Anja's tram had already started to rattle away when Frank looked up and saw it. He pushed Anja in its direction and she showed surprising agility as she leapt for the rear door just as the tram's momentum threatened to take it beyond her. In the process she dropped her satchel but Frank scooped it up and threw it close enough for her to reel it in. There was amused applause from a few passers-by.

As he retraced his steps Frank saw remnants of the previous day's parade, bits of coloured paper pushed up against shop walls or lying in gutters or swept into piles which the light breeze was already unravelling. A newsboy loomed up in front of him and waved a copy of the newspaper, his voice at fever pitch. Frank made to push past but as he did so he saw an oversized headline and a photograph of a large building on fire. He felt in his pocket for some coins but it was empty. He shook his head to apologise but the boy's attention was already elsewhere.

Frank's relief once he got inside off the street was cut short by the voices he heard. He had told them to be quiet, Frau Brekker would be sniffing around, but they obviously had not taken any notice. It was a wonder she was not beating down the door. But when he entered the room it was the landlady's voice he heard. She was talking animatedly to Max, as if she knew him. Frank caught Frau Wolters's name, then Father Klein's. He was intrigued, but he was distracted by the figure of Father Schapp, who was standing next to Frau Brekker and Max, his face pale and a thin film of perspiration on his forehead.

Father Schapp broke away from the circle and asked Frank whether Fräulein Auer was on her way home. 'Her father searched everywhere last night. He wanted to come here but they dragged him from his car and interrogated him. He has been through hell, the whole family.'

Frank started to explain about the search for a telephone and the beatings near the river and about Bill.

'The other young man?' Frau Brekker seemed to address the question to the room as a whole. She shuffled her feet as she spoke. Frank noticed she was wearing brightly-coloured slippers and fleetingly he conjured up an image of the parade, with its purity and exhilaration.

Max motioned to Jak to move. He took Jak's chair and placed it next to Frau Brekker, who sat down. But the rearrangement was immediately interrupted by the sound of muffled explosions, three or four dull concussions, discrete yet interlaced. Outside there were shouts, packets of sound that dispersed and dissolved.

Frau Brekker had her hands over her ears. Father Schapp looked at Max.

'You have nowhere else?'

'They know all our places, Father.'

'You can't burden Frau Brekker.'

There was a short, deep silence.

'There's the presbytery,' Father Schapp offered.

'He wants to save our souls,' Jak replied, almost inaudibly.

Frau Brekker rallied abruptly. 'The parishioners, Father?'

'Just until this fury has passed.'

'And if the fury has just begun?' Frau Brekker reddened, her own words seeming to embarrass or frighten her.

The air in the room was stale, the warmth of the bodies forming a heavy mixture with the limited artificial heat. Frank felt sweat on his back and shivered. Father Schapp helped Frau Brekker to her feet.

'Near Jakob Lane,' Father Schapp explained to Max. 'Frau Brekker will give you directions.'

'I know it, Father.'

'But wait until dark.'

The priest was at the door when he turned and said to Jak that he could not save his soul; only Jak himself could do that. 'With God's help.'

Frank suddenly remembered the newsboy. He announced, to no one in particular: 'The Reichstag has burned down.'

IV
The Church : March – April 1933

Wednesday 1 – Saturday 4 March 1933

The telephone in the presbytery rang again. It was Clemens Schapp, sounding at one moment like a representative of the Catholic Party, at another like a brother.

'They'll use it against us, Martin. You must understand that.'

Father Schapp responded that the young men would be beaten and thrown in jail, perhaps worse. And how had the news travelled so quickly to Berlin?

The question was ignored.

'They're not our people. Sometimes, the lesser evil.'

'Not our people?'

'You know very well what I mean.' Then after a pause: 'There's still a chance for us. Hitler is staking everything on next Sunday. If he fails to get a majority the Reichspresident will step in and send him packing and install a new cabinet. That's the rumour. It's our only chance. One last effort.'

Father Schapp remained silent and Clemens muttered in frustration that they would probably bring up again the business about the abuse of boys and surely Martin did not want that. The conversation petered out.

A short time later Michael telephoned from Düsseldorf. There would be an article on the Reichstag fire in the next edition of *The Vanguard* newspaper. There were rumours the Nazis had started it themselves, a cynical excuse to justify more oppression.

'They'll make a connection between us, Father. They'll say I sympathise with the communists. They'll use this to undermine what we publish.'

'Anja is here,' Father Schapp said, skirting around the impasse. 'She came looking for Frank and refuses to leave.'

Michael left a gap and Father Schapp explained that Frank and Stormy Weather had come to the presbytery late the previous night, bringing with them two suitcases full of clothing and books and other things for Max and Jak. And in their wake a truckload of brownshirts had descended on the presbytery, fretting and fuming and demanding access. He had resisted, he had argued they were not the police and had no authority, a hastily assembled group of parishioners had rallied around and the brownshirts had retreated, apart from a small contingent left to watch and harass.

'They will not violate this place,' Father Schapp declared.

—

Michael had said he would find a solution and that someone would telephone. When the call came Father Schapp thought he recognised the voice. He tried to put a face and name to it.

'Jochen, isn't it?'

'Any of the brownshirts still outside, Father?'

'I don't think so. I think they've gone.'

'It will be tonight then. We will create a diversion, just in case.'

'Some of my parishioners are standing guard.'

'Send them home, Father.'

'What time will it be?'

'I'll telephone beforehand.'

After the telephone call Father Schapp went outside and convinced the guarding parishioners there was no further need for their vigil. 'They would have acted by now. They have more important things to do.'

Inside the presbytery Jak could not keep still, he paced the full extent of the front room. Max sat quietly, smoking and cradling a cup of something hot. Both had several layers of clothing on. Anja and Frank were sitting together on the old sofa, hardly speaking, while Stormy was trying to read by the light of an old standard lamp. The suitcases stood ready in the corridor near the front door.

Father Schapp shuttled between his study and the front room. Several times he opened the front door, stepped outside and looked around the side of the building, walked further and surveyed the scrap of back yard, went to the front gate and assured himself that it was off the latch.

It was after midnight when the telephone rang again.

'Is everything clear, Father?'

'Yes.'

'In five minutes then.'

Max and Jak moved to the front door. The house lights were off. Frank went to the window and peered out. He could see little in the dim sheen of street light. Then a glow caught his attention, further along the street, at least a hundred yards away. He heard a dull crump and saw flames fan into the air. Then a second explosion, dull and gloomy, followed by a concert of disturbed night sounds. Then the sound of an engine approaching.

Suddenly the darkness in front of the presbytery began to twist and turn, silent shapes appeared and slid across Frank's vision, they crouched and waited. Frank heard the front door of the presbytery open. 'No!' he shouted.

Max was already running, eyes on the gate, suitcase in one hand, the other hand rehearsing opening motions.

At the front door Martin Schapp had both hands on Jak and was dragging him back inside while Jak's arms flailed about. The door was half open. There were shouts, dark figures were swirling around. Father Schapp pulled the door shut.

Jak was on all fours. He stretched out his arms and brought his head down towards his hands. He made a series of muted sounds then started to bang his forehead on the floor. Frank's heart was slamming into his ribcage. 'They were waiting, Father.'

—

Through the window Michael could see isolated figures walking with purpose on the zigzagging Düsseldorf streets, leaning forward and pushing themselves through the early morning. Inside it was perfectly still. No one had arrived yet, it was much too early.

He had been woken by a man he had never seen before, knocking quietly on his door in the pitch dark. 'They're raiding the Vanguard office,' the man had said and quickly disappeared.

When Michael got to the office signs of disturbance were everywhere. Typewriters had been taken, several cabinet drawers were open, papers were strewn around. And the article on the Reichstag fire, corrections and question marks in the margin, had disappeared from his desk. He sat down and tried to calm his nerves.

It was not just the raid that was tearing at him. He was still full of frustration and disbelief at Father Schapp's news of the betrayal. He had promised he would find out what had happened, he had spoken to Theo and Felix and several of the others but no one had heard from Jochen or knew where he was. He was left constructing alternative explanations for what had become obvious.

Some of the others had now arrived in the office and there were looks of bewilderment and consternation, questions about what it meant. Michael asked everyone to examine their area carefully to identify what had been taken. The result was as he had thought. They had taken things that were in their path. The only document of significance was the draft of the Reichstag fire article. He would have to write it out again. But it would not take long, it was all in his head.

In the middle of the morning two policemen came into the office. One of them asked Michael to state his name and to confirm that he was the editor of *The Vanguard*. He then handed Michael a sheet of paper. As he did so he stood to attention and declaimed: '*The Vanguard* may not be published until further notice, effective immediately. By order of the Interior Minister. Any violation of the order will be punished by imprisonment.'

The two policemen turned and left the office. Michael remembered when those uniforms with the rakish headwear had signified order and reassurance. Now they left him feeling impotent and humiliated.

—

Frank, Anja and Stormy walked to Frank and Bill's room. Frank collected clothes and wash things and piled them into his suitcase, along with a few books and his university assignments. He gave Stormy the key and said he could use the room and the kitchen for the time being.

He had not been going to take his bike but Anja said he should. And the radio as well. Anja carried the suitcase, changing it regularly from hand to hand, while Frank wheeled his bike with the radio balanced on the handle bars. Every now and then they stopped, Frank repositioned the radio, rested it and the bike against his body, stood and caught his breath while Anja sat on the suitcase and looked around. There was nothing untoward on the streets. It was a normal Saturday morning.

As they got near the presbytery they could see one of the parishioners, rugged up in an old coat, sitting on an upturned wooden box with a dog beside him. The dog was of medium size with a short grey coat and a scruffy beard. As they got closer it started to growl, but the man touched it and spoke to it softly and calmed it.

Without warning a pair of brownshirts appeared from the side of the building. It was too late to turn around so Frank and Anja kept moving, eyes straight ahead. But the brownshirts did not pay them any attention. Instead they busied themselves hammering a stake with a sign affixed into the ground. Frank stole a look and made out a denunciation of Father Schapp for harbouring communists, enemies of religion and of Germany, in crude, loud letters. And an appeal to the parishioners of St. Agnes's to stand up for their country and their faith.

Frank and Anja were at the presbytery door when one of the brownshirts called out: 'For the Führer's victory speech!' Frank turned and saw the owner of the voice laughing and pointing at the radio.

Father Schapp helped them to carry everything inside. They went into the front room where Jak was slumped on the floor, playing a card game with himself. Jak did not look up, but his relief that they were back was palpable. Frank had a strong sense that, in this room with these people, he was where he belonged.

Tuesday 21 March 1933

With each passing day the brown miasma spread more widely and deeply. Anja and Frank avoided the main mensa, they went to the smaller mensa frequented by the orientalists, but it soon took on the prevailing colour and mood. Nowhere was safe. Frank found his access to a class blocked by a guard of brownshirted students insisting it was his patriotic duty to boycott the lecturer. He stumbled past, not taking in what was happening, escaping with a mild jostling. The next time he summoned his strength to run the gauntlet but there was no one there. 'All lectures by the Jew Aaronsohn cancelled', a sign on the door said. Another sign said: 'The Jew knows only how to lie!'

Each time they ventured out, the two of them on Frank's bike, wobbling and swaying, Anja sitting sideways on the crossbar with Frank's arms around her, he felt a shiver of fear that they might never be able to return. Not that they would be arrested and interrogated and beaten, although he occasionally tried to imagine what that would be like. His fear was that a wall of brownshirts would build itself around the presbytery while they were gone and seal it off. He imagined Jak and Father Schapp inside, himself and Anja outside, with no chance of communication apart from a desperate glance through the front room window.

He had been mooning around the presbytery one day when Father Schapp handed him a newspaper. It was a Catholic periodical, published in Munich, in recent months twice a week. There had been one edition since the election at the beginning of March, but since then nothing. 'The editor has been arrested,' Father Schapp had been told on the telephone. 'Pray for him, Father.'

Frank had never been one for newspapers, he preferred stories and poetry, but this paper fascinated him. He had started with the most recent issue and gone backwards to the beginning of the year, then into the previous year, the intricate Gothic script making extra demands on his concentration. So much that had been opaque now became clear. It would take him an hour to read one of the longer articles. Then he would get up and walk around the front room, go to the kitchen, cut himself a piece of bread and spread a thin layer of jam on it, make something hot to drink, go to the window and draw back the curtains and look outside. Occasionally he would try to talk to Jak or Anja about what he had read, but they showed little interest. So he would imagine himself talking to his father, explaining what was at stake. 'Everything's at stake,' he said out loud one day. He lifted his head to see Anja give him a curious look. He remembered Jak's words. 'The most serious thing in the world.'

After the election the previous July the newspaper had been banned for four weeks. It had published an article making fun of the Nazi race theories, suggesting that the leader himself had Mongolian blood. Later there had been a series of articles discussing negotiations between the Catholic Party and the Nazis on forming a coalition. Frank was shocked; he could hardly believe it. The paper was very critical and Frank instinctively cheered it on, barracking like at a football match, right up to the time when the negotiations foundered and new themes appeared, much to his relief, even though it was all in the past.

Anja would occasionally pick up one of the newspapers and flick through the pages. There were advertisements that would attract her attention, for motion pictures or for leisurely chauffeur-driven car journeys through the Bavarian countryside. 'Let's do that, Frank, the two of us. Like a king and queen.' And for trips to Rome, including an audience with the Pope. 'What would you say to the Holy Father, if you had the chance?' Frank could not think of anything and Anja said she would tell the Holy Father he should stop listening to his advisers and come to Germany and see for himself what the Nazis were really like.

When Michael unexpectedly appeared in the front room, ushered in by Father Schapp, Frank was immersed in an issue of the paper from May 1932. There had been rumours that the Catholic Party's Heinrich Brüning would be replaced as Reichschancellor and the paper was discussing the good and bad of his time in office. The balance was not in his favour. Frank had formed a positive impression of Herr Brüning, from scraps of information and a predisposition to think well of a Catholic chancellor. He had in his imagination someone sincere, honest and upright, holding back the tide. It was unpleasant to have this impression undermined and he resisted what he was reading, looking for chinks in the argument.

Anja was lying on the floor, toying with the radio. She was twisting the dial one way then the other, producing squealing and whooping sounds that Frank was doing his best to ignore.

'For heaven's sake stop that,' Michael snapped, then seemed immediately to regret his words. 'Please.'

Anja did as she was asked. She looked up at her brother but said nothing.

Michael and Frank exchanged handshakes. Michael went to Anja and squatted next to her.

'Papa isn't well. The doctor has ordered him to bed.' He brushed a strand of hair from Anja's face. 'Papa needs you at home.'

The scene was interrupted by urgent voices from outside. The presbytery's door flew open and two men stumbled into the hall, carrying a body. They laid their load down on the floor.

'We found him in Jakob Lane, Father,' one of the men said between gasps. 'He needs a doctor.'

Frank gasped at the sight of Max Wolters, lying unconscious, his face bruised and bloodied, his shirt torn and his feet bare.

A few brownshirts were milling around the front door. One of them poked his head inside and tried to assert himself. 'Today a great event will take place in Potsdam. A great day in the reawakening of our country.' Father Schapp slammed the door shut.

Jak appeared and helped the men to move Max to the presbytery's bedroom, where Anja took over, answering her womanly calling to minister to the injured man.

Frank thought of Frau Wolters, of what she had said about her son. *Dead in some stinking ditch.* He should telephone her. But he did not want to talk to Father Klein.

Father Schapp was at the side of the bed. He whispered to Max that he would get a message to his mother, then left the room.

A moment of anxious quiet was disrupted by a gash of noise from the front room. Crowds were cheering, drums beating and music lashing. A feeling of unreality overtook Frank. He looked at Jak for an explanation but saw only blankness. Then Anja told him to go and turn off the radio.

A single voice was issuing forth, rising and falling, at first difficult to decipher, then triumphantly riding a wave of cheering, of drum beats and band music. *'You can hear, German listeners, the calls of acclamation. Such unbounded enthusiasm. What a wonderful, wonderful day, this day of Potsdam. To the right the army, to the left the brown rows of the nationalist movement. Unprecedented enthusiasm.'*

Frank strained to understand. The voice disappeared into the background, the drum beats kept pounding. He thought he could hear church bells. He saw young faces peering in through the window, enthralled, spellbound.

'The opening of the new parliament.' Michael was explaining, without taking his attention from the broadcast. 'Blatant appeal to nationalist feeling. The old Prussian nationalists, the new National Socialists. But they're doing it well.'

The voice on the radio pushed itself to ever higher levels of fervour. *'And now the young German chancellor, Herr Adolf Hitler, raises his hand in greeting. German listeners, hear the enthusiasm. Unprecedented...a whole people, a rousing commitment to the renewal of the nation at the grave of Frederick the Great...millions upon millions of people, who in this moment see their whole longing realised. Hope with us, believe with us, German listeners...and now the Reichspresident, the Field Marshall, the Chancellor bows, offers his hand. Unprecedented enthusiasm.'*

The background noise disappeared and a single voice intoned. Jak appeared in the doorway, the blankness in his face replaced by hostility.

'I dissolved the previous parliament in order to give the German people the opportunity to pass judgment on the new government of national unity. The election has given this government a clear majority and created a constitutional basis for its work.'

Frank was struck by the firmness and clarity of the voice. From what he knew about the Reichspresident he was expecting something feeble and doddering.

'...to look back at the old Prussia...to free ourselves from selfishness...'

Frank looked up and saw Father Schapp hurrying in from outside. He was carrying a chalice in one hand and a small container in the other. 'The last rites,' Frank wondered, but the radio intervened.

'...*a united, free and proud Germany. And now I hand over to the Reichschancellor.*'

Anja was suddenly in the room. 'Turn if off, Michael,' she pleaded. There was a lull and Anja whispered forlornly into the stillness. 'Father tried to give Max communion, but he could not swallow. So he put some wine on his lips.'

The new voice on the radio was calm to begin with. For several seconds Frank was not sure it was *him*. But then came the familiar themes, the injustice of the World War, the ignominy of Versailles, the destruction of the nation's self-belief, the unemployment. And throughout their history the German people seeking refuge in an internal world, the world of the poet and the thinker, dreaming of a world that for other nations was reality.

A memory of Bill Parker in the mensa cut across the speech. 'This country promises a special seriousness, a greater depth of experience. But it is probably an illusion.'

Frank tried to refocus but heard only isolated words and phrases: '...*unshakeable will...awakening...life struggle...*' Then a string of words caught his attention, '...*national self-determination and spiritual renewal...*', and despite himself he felt a quiver go through his body, a glimmer of vicarious pride. Then the threatening tone returned. '*And those who seek to harm our people we will render harmless.*'

Father Schapp entered the room. 'I think that's enough, Michael,' he suggested.

'*The government of national renewal is determined to fulfil the task it has been given by the German people.*'

Applause resounded, wave upon wave, threatening to overtax the radio's capacity, stretching its membranes to breaking point. Then the tide ebbed and Father Schapp said into the quiet. 'Max is gone.'

For several moments there was a desperate calm. Then a flood of curses poured from Jak's mouth. He strode to the radio, kicked at it. He wrenched the plug from the wall, then went to the window and slammed it shut.

Father Schapp quietly proposed a prayer for the repose of Max's soul. He knelt and the others followed, apart from Jak, who paced up and down and kicked out again at the radio.

'Let us pray that God will release Max from his sins and make a place for him in His company. Eternal rest grant unto him O Lord, and let perpetual light shine upon him.'

'Amen.'

A hesitant peace settled on the room. Even Jak's turbulence seemed for the time being to have played itself out. Father Schapp went to each of Anja and Frank and Jak in turn and laid a hand on their shoulders.

There was a knock on the door and Michael went to answer it. He returned with Stormy Weather, who was out of breath and agitated.

'Some of the shops have radios playing but there are large crowds and I could not get close enough to hear.'

Stormy looked inquiringly at the silent radio. Then he took a letter out of his pocket and handed it to Frank. 'Frau Brekker has been keeping this, waiting for your return.'

Frank opened the letter but he could not bring himself to read the contents.

'There's a throng out the front,' Stormy said, his tone questioning.

Father Schapp went to the window and drew aside the curtain. He turned back to the room. 'I asked some of the parishioners to come, just in case. There has been a good response.'

Frank looked out the window. The scene momentarily reminded him of a weekend working bee at the church at home, the men of the parish giving up their Saturday morning to clean the yard and repair the buildings. Through the memory he was reminded of the letter in his hand. He unfolded the page and began to read.

—

Mum is still very weak. She can't do much with her right arm and she's wobbly on her pins. The girls are doing their best, Ellie especially, very grown up, and Margie's been good too. But your mother is constantly asking for you. She doesn't understand the delay.

Frank bent down and picked up a scrap of paper which had fallen to the floor, on one side Margie's distinctive scrawl.

Ellie thinks she can boss me around and Daddy and Mummy don't do anything about it. I couldn't go to the beach much during the holidays and it was so hot in the house. My teacher this year is Mrs. Dunn and I don't like her. I hate school this year. Please come home soon.

—

Frank lifted his head towards Anja but she was staring vacantly into space. He looked around the room and wondered who the people were and why he was there. Then two men in white tunics appeared in the doorway and said they had come to collect a body.

Father Schapp was quickly on his feet, leading the men to the bedroom. Michael and Stormy and Frank stood up, almost at attention.

'...*the grey rows of the Reichswehr in firm step march past the Reichschancellor...the Field Marshall saluting...oh German listeners, a wonderful, wonderful day...*'

The radio had defiantly sprung back to life and Jak again lashed out at it. Father Schapp put his head into the room. 'They are taking Max now.'

The two men in white carried a stretcher with Max's body, covered by a crumpled sheet. Father Schapp held the front door open.

The group of parishioners at the front of the presbytery numbered about a dozen, mostly men in their sixties. They easily outweighed the handful of brownshirts in size and in years, but that did not stop the latter from directing taunts at them. It was on the radio, the President and the Chancellor, the old and the new, if they had heard it their hearts would be beating proudly. The Catholic Party members of parliament were all there. There was no reason now to stand aside from the new Germany.

The occupants of the presbytery followed Max outside and Father Schapp let the door close and joined them. The parishioners moved this way and that to form a rough and ready honour guard, to which a few of the brownshirts tentatively and incongruously added themselves.

When the small procession had almost reached the front gate Jak let out a keening sound that seemed to stretch the air to breaking point. When the spasm passed Frank looked around and his gaze came to rest on the scruffy dog which was a regular part of the presbytery's guard. It was stretched out on the ground with a young brownshirt squatting at its side, stroking its neck and whispering in its ear.

An ambulance stood at the kerb, its back doors wide open in a grim gesture of welcome. The attendants eased the stretcher into the cavity, fixed it in place and closed the doors with hardly a sound. With a curt nod in the direction of Father Schapp they were gone.

As the vehicle disappeared a pair of figures emerged from the glare, walking towards the presbytery. Frank recognised Father Klein and Frau Wolters.

Friday 24 & Sunday 26 March 1933

'Those things have no place here. You have no place here.' Father Schapp's words were clear and steady, his voice raised just enough to find its target.

All eyes were now focused on the rear of the church, where a troop of Nazis were arrayed in crisp brown uniforms, with swastika flags and sashes, splashes of red, white and black. Frank widened his gaze and saw Ernst Tüchnow and Arnie Wriedt and some of those who had been stationed outside the presbytery. The one who had fixed his bike, Gerd, fidgeting and smirking, and nearby Bobby O'Donnell and his retinue. Not in uniform, but Bobby with a Nazi armband, looking admiringly at Ernst.

'Have you not been following events in Berlin, Father?' Ernst was full of confidence. 'Now even the Catholic Party is with us.'

'The Archbishop has forbidden you and your symbols to enter our churches. I must ask you to leave.'

As Father Schapp was speaking a number of male parishioners stood up and edged their way into the aisle and moved to the back of the church. Frank recognised some of the presbytery guard but most were younger, strapping figures with broad shoulders and deep chests evident under their Sunday suits. As they moved they separated into two groups, each five or six strong, and stationed themselves at the ends of the pews where Ernst and his troop were gathered.

'You should treat our presence as an offer of reconciliation. In the interests of the Fatherland.'

Before Ernst had finished one of the men took the nearest brownshirt by the elbow. 'Time to go.'

Despite his size Gerd Neumann allowed himself to be manoeuvred aside. Arnie Wriedt let his flag drop from its vertical position and pointed the sharp end at one of the parishioners. Other brownshirts followed suit. Scuffles broke out, a punch was thrown and a melee started to develop. But then it stopped, arrested by the sound of Father Schapp's voice, intoning a Latin prayer. The opposed groups disentangled, stood back from each other and set their clothes to rights. 'I will go unto the altar of God,' Father Schapp continued.

The congregation turned back to the front of the church. Its response to Father Schapp's words was a thin veneer over the sound of creaking wood and rustling clothes. 'To God, Who gives joy to my youth.'

—

Friday had been a joyless day of cold and wind and rain. Frank had attended Max's funeral at St. Benedict's, he thought he owed that to Frau Wolters and to Max, but the anonymity he had hoped for had been thwarted by the paucity of the congregation, a handful of aging women who had left him and Father Schapp to support Frau Wolters. The ceremony itself was eerie, the prayers and hymns overpowered by the resounding organ. And Father Klein's sermon was awkward, the meagre consolation it offered to the bereaved swept away by an evocation of grave threats and forbidding perils that only a reawakened Fatherland and absolute faith in God could combat.

After Mass the inner circle accompanied the coffin to a far corner of the Catholic cemetery, where the two priests prayed in unison in the scudding wind and Frau Wolters steadied herself against Frank as Max's body was lowered into the ground. The promise of eternity sat uneasily in Frank's mind alongside the clammy sensation of the soil which fell from his hand into the grave.

'It's a good thing you've done, Father.' As Frau Wolters spoke to Father Klein the group shifted on its feet and prepared to move away.

When they returned to the presbytery Frau Wolters busied herself preparing something to eat and drink, but she did not join the others at the kitchen table. She said she was exhausted and needed to rest.

Father Klein was the first to speak after Frau Wolters had gone. 'The Archbishop was not in favour, but I could not disappoint Frau Wolters.'

Father Schapp moved his hands apart to indicate that he understood. But he seemed reluctant to put this agreement into words.

Father Klein moved to another subject. 'The Catholic Party has made a wise decision.'

Frank looked for clarification and Father Klein explained. 'The leaders of our Party have agreed to allow the Chancellor to rule without recourse to parliament. They have placed their trust in the new government, in the future.'

'The bishops have not yet spoken,' Father Schapp responded.

In the quiet that followed Frank could feel the balance of power between the two priests shift. The longer the silence lasted the stronger Father Klein appeared.

'The Catholic Party is not the Church,' Frank suggested. But this invitation to restart the debate was ignored. Instead Father Klein raised a telephone call he had received from Frank's father. 'He asked me to speak to you. He told me you are needed at home. Your mother is ill. He does not understand the delay.'

Frank was caught off guard. All he could think to say was that he had come too far to go back now. Then he fell into an embarrassed silence.

'I understand,' Father Klein said. 'You do not wish to forego the opportunity you have been given to witness the rebirth of a great nation.'

After this solemn proclamation the priest sat back in his chair and began to smile, his large face unfolding and opening like a flower in new sunlight. Frank was taken aback by the appearance of such grace in features so unprepossessing.

—

Frank looked at Anja. He could see and feel her disappointment. He looked away. He allowed himself to fall in with the rhythm of the Mass, then found his mind turning to what Father Schapp should say in his sermon. He remembered the strong words from the Catholic newspaper and rehearsed them in his head. Racial exclusion, worship of violence and of false gods, trenchantly opposed by the Holy Roman Catholic Church, an expression of spirit and peace and love, the final bulwark against an unconditional evil. He steeled himself, clenched his muscles and tightened his will. He felt pressure from Anja's hand. He looked down and caught her questioning look, then dropped his head and adopted the posture of prayer.

But the attempted prayer did not take root. Instead Frank found himself thinking about Max and Bill and death. He tried to imagine himself not existing, but no matter which approach he took he was still there, imagining. *And if I could somehow succeed in thinking myself out of existence? I would take the world with me, there would be nothing left. But this cannot be right.* He wondered what Stormy would say. He looked at his friend, standing between Anja and Jak, but Stormy seemed withdrawn, as if intent on allowing the sights and sounds and smells of the Mass to imprint themselves unhindered on his senses.

Frank focused on Father Schapp, seeking reassurance in the familiarity of the priest's words and gestures. But his attention wavered and Father Klein's smile from the day of Max's funeral began to insinuate itself into his mind, and its sincerity and purity unsettled him. The rebirth of a great nation. Could that be true?

—

Father Schapp was thinking about his sermon. He had prepared carefully, put in hours of concentration, but the message was simple. My brothers and sisters in Christ, we should not be distracted by the tactics of our politicians. Berlin is far away, and who really understands the intrigues of that world? Let us listen above all to the leaders of the Church, to our cardinals, archbishops and bishops. They have spoken clearly in the past and they will speak clearly again. Rest assured that if in future members of the National Socialist movement are welcomed into our churches, it will mean that their doctrines and their behaviour have changed. It will not mean that the Church has changed.

Father Schapp said this from the pulpit when he finally found his way there. He made no mention of Ernst Tüchnow and his group, averting his gaze even as their presence dug into his insides and scraped at his nerves. He spoke to his people, to the devout Catholics who God had given into his care. At that moment he had no doubt about the truth of what he was saying. He felt its truth as surely as he felt his own self at the centre of his being. It was just a matter of finding the right words to communicate this feeling, to make this commitment to truth, this refusal to compromise with evil, irresistible. When he turned to leave the pulpit he felt he had succeeded.

As he made his way back to the altar the feeling of accomplishment was replaced by the memory of his brother's voice on the telephone, shot through with hesitation and tears as he recounted what had happened in the Reichstag. The leaders of the Catholic Party had argued for acquiescence to the Reichschancellor's demands, they had cajoled and threatened those colleagues who were holding out. A refusal would see renewed persecution of Catholics, while cooperation would be rewarded with a concordat, a formal agreement between the Reich and the Vatican. The Church's place in the new order would be secured. But Clemens was under no illusion. 'The Reichstag voted itself out of existence. And we Catholics said "Amen".'

—

Frank could not kneel any longer and he pushed his backside onto the seat, feeling relief as the pain in his knees abated. Jak was sitting beside Anja with his hands in his pockets and his body hunched. He had not gone to communion with Frank and the others, he had hardly moved the whole time. When the congregation stood, when it knelt, Jak had stayed sitting, seemingly oblivious to the glances directed at him.

Near the end of the queue approaching the altar rail Frank could see Arnie Wriedt and Ernst Tüchnow and some other brownshirts. Bobby O'Donnell was there too, a study in affected piety. As Ernst's group knelt at the altar rail Frank stretched his neck so he could see better. He was not the only one straining to see. Heads were darting this way and that.

Father Schapp took a host from the chalice, made a small sign of the cross, murmured the words 'the body and blood of Christ' and then bent to place the host on the outstretched tongue. When his eyes caught sight of the uniform his arm stopped its movement and he motioned to the altar boy, whose hand holding the metal plate under Ernst Tüchnow's chin was shaking wildly, to move to the next communicant. But Tüchnow's left hand shot out and took firm hold of the priest's wrist, his right hand following. Frank forgot himself and half stood to watch the test of strength. Ernst had the advantage, both elbows propped on the altar rail. He pulled Father Schapp's arm down, took the host in his lips and manoeuvred it onto his tongue and then swallowed. He made the sign of the cross and got to his feet, slowly and deliberately.

Father Schapp stood still, gathering himself. Then he turned and walked back to the altar, followed by the trembling altar boy, leaving the remaining brownshirts, Bobby O'Donnell among them, empty-handed but smirking at the altar rail.

They ate lunch together, pressed up against each other at the kitchen table. Frank had withdrawn more money from the bank and given it to one of the women responsible for preparing meals, so there was enough food to fill their stomachs. As usual Jak led the way in demonstrating enthusiasm for the meal by means of an array of guttural noises and sharp gesticulations. But even he was less boisterous than normal. There was hardly any talk.

Finally Father Schapp said: 'It has been wonderful having you all here. But now it is time to go. The Nazis have made their point. They won't be back.' He waited, perhaps hoping for objections, but none came, just some masticated words from Jak about a last supper.

The gathering broke up and there was a general collecting of possessions and a replacing of pieces of furniture in initial positions. Then everyone assembled in the front room, which took on the air of a waiting room in a railway station, until they heard the car arrive.

A soft light greeted the little group as it made its way outside. It settled around them and seemed to accompany them like a halo. The occasional voices of passers-by and their footsteps were clearly audible. Friedrich Auer was standing at the door of the car and he directed Frank into the front passenger seat. Anja climbed into the back seat and Jak squeezed in beside her with his suitcase.

'I have kept your daughter too long, Herr Auer.' Father Schapp was standing next to the older man. 'Please forgive me.'

'Are we surrendering without a fight, Father?'

'We should wait for the bishops. They will speak clearly.'

When the car had gone Father Schapp and Stormy Weather went back inside the presbytery. At Father Schapp's insistence the women who cleaned for him were spending the afternoon with their families, so the kitchen had to be tidied, things washed and put away. The priest ran water into the sink to signal the beginning of the task. Stormy found a tea towel and he dried things and stacked them carefully. He had questions about the Mass, about belief and doubt and certainty, but Father Schapp seemed turned in on himself and uninterested in conversation.

Wednesday 29 March 1933

Frank had gone to Father Schapp's presbytery to collect his bike and had accepted an invitation to eat and drink something. Stormy was at the kitchen table, surrounded by the remnants of a meal, acting as if his continued presence required no explanation. When Frank and Father Schapp sat down Stormy resumed a conversation.

'I have been watching you at the altar, Father.'

The priest was fingering a newspaper on the table beside him. 'I can feel your eyes on me. I feel I need to be on my best behaviour.'

'I have been wondering what goes through your mind. When you lift the host into the air and raise your head. I understand this is the pinnacle.'

'I try to keep my mind empty. Empty for God.'

'My culture claims to have a high opinion of emptiness. But I have never been able to achieve it. I understand that the harder you try the more difficult it is. But then, I am not sure of the point.'

'The point?'

A telephone started to ring in another room. Martin Schapp stood up but he did not leave the kitchen. He leant against his chair, then sat down and picked up the newspaper. The ringing finally stopped. 'I'm sorry Tsutomu. Please excuse me.'

The priest read for a few moments then let the newspaper fall. The telephone started to ring again and he quickly got to his feet and went to answer it.

—

Stormy leant forward and read, then he pushed the paper towards Frank. He spoke softly as he did so.

'There was a large band of Nazis in church this morning. They were brandishing copies of the newspaper. They were in very high spirits.'

'Statement of the Catholic Bishops', the heading said. Frank skimmed the article, then laid the newspaper on the table and picked it up again. There were qualifications, admonitions that remained in force. But one sentence left no doubt what it all meant. 'Without reversing the condemnation of certain religious and moral errors which is contained in our former measures, the episcopate believes that it can be confident that the general prohibitions and warnings issued previously no longer need to be considered necessary.'

Frank asked in a parched voice: 'What will Father Schapp do now?'

—

'You've seen the statement, Father?'

'Just now, Michael.'

'There are qualifications. We should focus on these.'

'Have you spoken to Father Weidemeier?'

'He says it is an imprimatur. All we can do now is infiltrate their organisations, tame their excesses, turn their energy and patriotism into a force for good.'

'What do you think, Michael?'

The conversation faltered. Each man started to speak but only sentence fragments were audible. Then Martin Schapp said: 'They will come for you now. At first with blandishments, then with bared teeth. Like a pack of wolves.'

'We have our places, Father, secret places.'

There was a long pause, then a new subject.

'Your father looked frail.'

'He is much better. Now that Anja is home.'

'I miss Anja, and the others. But the young Japanese man is still here. He is very disciplined, putting every thought into proper alignment. I suppose it does me good.' Father Schapp added as an afterthought: 'And just now Frank has come.'

'Are the Nazis leaving you in peace, Father?'

'They were at Mass this morning, full of jubilation. An affront to us all.'

—

During her stay Anja had been given the presbytery's bedroom, and her lingering smell now added to Father Schapp's sense of abandonment. A deep exhaustion threatened to submerge him. It was as if for months or even years each passing day had deposited a layer of tiredness that no amount of sleep had been able to expunge.

He removed his jacket and untied his stock and undid his collar, laying each item out neatly on the bed. He took off his shoes and socks, then his black trousers, placing them carefully aside. He rested his hand on the discarded jacket and let his fingers smooth the lapels.

There were some old clothes in the wardrobe. He put on a pair of corduroy trousers, a heavy cotton shirt, a pullover with a high neck, thick socks and a pair of sturdy boots with mud caked around the soles. Then he went outside to the little piece of back yard. He dragged open the door of a rickety wooden shed which housed a collection of garden tools and groped around inside until he felt the smooth handle of a mattock. He tightened his hand and lifted it out.

Running along the back of the presbytery was a garden bed in which each summer he planted a few vegetables. Now it was just a patch of hard earth in deep shade, still with a faint dusting of frost. He walked over to it, braced his feet, lifted the mattock and swung. The tool shuddered as it hit the ground, sending a sharp shock into his hands and wrists. He lifted it again, swivelled it so the pick end faced down, aimed at the same spot and swung. This time the earth parted and he had to shake and twist the mattock handle to free the head. He stood up, already panting from the exertion, then resumed the task, lifting, swinging, opening up the ground, bending to pick up bits of earth, dropping them and breaking them with the heel of his boot. He could feel beads of sweat on his back, aching in his shoulders, the beginnings of a blister on his hand. But he kept on, lifting and swinging, relaxing his muscles to buffer each jarring shock as the mattock hit the hard earth.

He tried not to think. He wanted to leave his mind empty, empty for God. But he could not stop the chattering. About the sensations in his body. About Frank's radio, still squatting there in the front room. 'A wonderful, wonderful day.' About the bishops' capitulation, their betrayal. He did not want to believe it, but he knew it was true, even inevitable. He swung the mattock with maximum force. Its head caught in the ground and he overbalanced and almost fell.

Frank stood in the half-opened door. He waited for the priest to acknowledge his presence, but Martin Schapp remained absorbed in his actions. Eventually Frank called out: 'The telephone will not stop ringing, Father. And a group of parishioners has come. They would like to speak to you.'

The priest was taken aback by the term of address. In these clothes and in this attitude he felt himself not quite a priest. He forced himself to answer. 'Not now, Frank. I'll talk to them later. And you can disconnect the telephone.'

Frank pulled the door shut and disappeared inside. Martin Schapp went back to wielding the mattock.

Sunday 2 April 1933

The nine o'clock Mass was always the most popular. Seven o'clock was too early for all but the hardiest, especially with winter not yet fully gone, and eleven o'clock meant that when you got home it was already afternoon. Nine o'clock was the high point, like a football match between teams at the top of the table. And Father Schapp was right. They had come, and in numbers.

Michael had returned to Siebenkirchen the previous day for a short visit and Father Schapp had shown him the instructions on practical matters that had been sent to the clergy following the bishops' public statement. At first Michael could not see a way through. But then his attention came to rest on a single sentence, a condition on access to the sacraments. This was to be granted only to those for whom there were no well-grounded misgivings about their worthiness.

'There are misgivings about Tüchnow and the others, Father. They are implicated in the taking of innocent lives.'

'What do you have in mind, Michael?'

'They'll back down. If we show strength, they'll back down.'

On his way to the presbytery that morning Michael had made a detour through the old town, in search of distraction and a chance to assemble his thoughts. He had stopped outside Weiss's second-hand bookshop, his attention arrested at first by a hastily daubed Star of David on the window and then by a World War bravery medal draped over a triangle of display books. He had swallowed back his emotion and then stood and watched as a steady flow of customers entered and left the shop, ignoring the boycott, refusing to be intimidated, sidestepping a knot of snarling brownshirts at the front door. One woman had even brought a bouquet of flowers.

Michael had been tempted to taunt the Nazis, to tell them they were obviously wasting their time, but he had thought better of it and mounted his bike and pushed off hard, making light work of the cobblestones.

'That's if they even come,' Michael added.

But Father Schapp was in no doubt. 'They'll come.'

—

Michael was at the front of the church with most of the other Vanguarders arrayed around him. Frank and Jak and Felix were standing a little to one side, Felix's guitar case on the ground next to him. Anja was with them, rocking nervously from one leg to the other, trying to avoid Michael's line of sight.

Everyone had been surprised when August Langscheid had appeared not long before, peddling slowly but purposefully towards the church. He had told them the previous evening that his father's job was under threat, any false move and his father would be dismissed, he did not think he could come. He had been in tears and had left the meeting early, a few words of encouragement and understanding following him out of the room. But now he was there, linking arms with Theo and Harald.

Michael had promised his father that Anja would not be involved, and during the meeting he had told Frank and Jak that this was not a matter for them. The three friends had sat there in stony silence, but afterwards they had whispered their resolve to ignore Michael. Anja and Frank had their bikes, and Jak could take Lukas's. Anja had even asked Cordie if she wanted to come, but had not waited for an answer.

'Move aside please. We have every right to be here.' Ernst Tüchnow stood directly in front of Michael.

'The Mass is no place for political demonstrations.'

'You are the one demonstrating, Auer, in violation of the explicit instructions of the bishops. Now move aside.'

Ernst's retinue was over a dozen strong. There were those who had at various times during the preceding weeks kept watch outside the presbytery, and there were a number of new faces, some not much more than boys, a few older ones with substantial bodies. Bobby O'Donnell was there too, but there was no sign of Charles Smith or Ray Wright. There were uniforms, flags, bunting, all the trimmings. The first hymn had finished, the sound of the organ had folded itself away. Everything was in readiness.

Then a single word rang out, causing Ernst to stall and Michael to jerk back his head.

'Jochen?'

It was Felix who had spotted him, standing apart from the others, next to a car at the kerbside.

As he spoke Felix picked up his guitar case and started to walk toward the road, the mass of bodies parting sufficiently to allow him passage. He called Jochen's name again. At first Jochen seemed unsure and hesitant, but then he gathered himself and walked forward and held out his hand.

'You're with them,' Felix stated, ignoring the outstretched hand. He stood there looking and waiting, but Jochen said nothing. Instead he withdrew his hand and shrugged his shoulders and edged past Felix towards his new comrades.

The opposing groups outside the church, which had come to a standstill during this episode, returned to life. Ernst stepped forward and Michael used both hands to resist him. A general pushing and shoving began, a grabbing for fistfuls of clothing. The church door opened and the sound of Father Schapp's voice spilt out. The door closed and the sounds of the Mass disappeared.

Into the vacuum Jak hurled himself at Arnie Wriedt. He produced a knife and struggled to get his hand free to wield it, panting that this was for Bill and for Max. But Michael and a few of the others were there to wrench the knife away. Jak and Arnie were separated and the opposing contingents stood back from each other.

Jak stumbled away and Anja went and put her arms around him. Frank joined in and the three of them stood pressed together, shuffling their feet for balance, fighting with their tears.

The next movement came from Ernst Tüchnow, who picked up a discarded flag and walked quietly and unimpeded to the front door of the church. He stood there and briefly surveyed the scene, then opened the door and stepped inside. The other brownshirts soon followed. They marched into the vestibule and on with increasing swagger, past the holy water font and the niche with a statue of the Virgin Mary and beneath it a rack of candles, tiny flames shuddering in the disturbed air, into the body of the church where they were met by Father Schapp's voice. 'They set up their abominations in the house, which is called by my name, to defile it.' The congregation increased its density to accommodate the newcomers.

Outside, the Vanguarders struggled to maintain formation. They were looking to Michael. Harald and Felix were standing next to him but the others were hanging back. Jochen was waiting at the church door and first Ollie and then Carl broke away and went in his direction. August and Theo soon followed, stealing glances at Michael to see how he would react, whether he would call them to order. But he had turned his back and was preparing to leave.

Anja told Frank to fetch his bike, they should leave with Michael. Frank asked where they would go to Mass, but Anja ignored the question. She motioned to Jak to accompany her.

Frank hesitated, looking at the church. Anja grabbed his arm. 'We can't go in there, Frank. Not with them.'

Frank eased his arm free. 'The bishops have withdrawn their objections,' he stammered.

Anja's face shifted and contorted and Frank recognised the look of disgust from the mensa. At first he thought it was directed at the bishops, but then he realised it was meant for him.

'Wait!' he called.

Anja was moving away, wheeling her bicycle. When she reached the street she stopped and turned. 'If you go in there I will never speak to you again.'

Frank felt an intense desire to submit, but something in him refused. He called out that they should support Father Schapp, after all he had done for them. But even as he spoke he knew that Father Schapp was not the reason for his resistance. If it were just a choice between individuals, he would choose Anja.

For several long seconds there was a standoff, Anja refusing to concede any ground, Frank reacting stubbornly to her refusal. Then Anja engaged her pedals and wobbled away, with Jak alongside her. Frank remained where he was until the figures disappeared, then walked on leaden legs towards the church, his journey punctuated by backward looks.

—

Inside the church the air was heavy with organ chords and human voices. Frank took a deep breath and squinted into the dim light. He could not see the Vanguarders, they seemed to have melted into the human mass, but the brownshirts were unmistakable, congregated in several knots of colour and self-satisfaction. He looked away and his gaze fell on Stormy Weather, standing perfectly still and tight-lipped at the aisle end of a nearby pew. He took a few quick steps and squeezed himself in beside Stormy, who silently acknowledged his presence by yielding a little space.

When the hymn finished the congregation took some time to settle. But as Father Schapp reached the pulpit the nervous rustling fell silent.

'An expression of absolute goodness and love,' Frank remembered, as Father Schapp stood looking down on the congregation, composing himself. 'A final bulwark against an unconditional evil.' But his face seems thinner, his hair greyer.

Father Schapp spread his arms. 'My Dearly Beloved in Christ.'

A baby cried into the open space. 'Don't worry, Frau Hartmann,' Father Schapp said. 'I'll drown it out.' A smattering of laughter briefly eased the tension. The woman carried her baby to the back of the church, and Father Schapp resumed.

'Our German Fatherland stands before challenges that are perhaps the most difficult in its history, more difficult even than those of war. And it is right that to meet these challenges we should stand together. The bishops have therefore called for reconciliation. They have instructed us to put aside enmity and animosity, to welcome those who have been our enemies. Of course we must obey.'

The congregation breathed out, then watched as a small number of worshippers stood in ones and twos and manoeuvred their way to the end of the creaking seats, genuflected and strode down the aisle and out of the church. Among those leaving were several of the men who had kept watch outside the presbytery, and Frank could imagine Anja's voice insisting that he join them, declaring that this was his last chance. But he remained still, his mind spinning.

Father Schapp seemed spent, close to tears. In response someone began to applaud and others joined in. Several stood in a show of support, Ernst Tüchnow and Bobby O'Donnell prominent among them. The action reached a plateau and then quickly fell away, leaving an embarrassed silence.

'But we must remain vigilant,' Father Schapp said, reasserting control. 'If our political leaders break their promises, if they violate the Word of God, we will resist them. The Church will resist. Let us take comfort from this knowledge.'

The priest returned to the altar and began preparations for the next phase of the Mass. The congregation knelt in ragged order to pray. Frank could sense around him a confused atmosphere of relief and disappointment, excitement and despondency, belief and doubt. Father Schapp raised his voice in prayer and the movement and the murmuring stilled, leaving Frank sitting alone, gripped by Anja's look and his own foreboding.

Could the rebirth of a great nation look and feel like this?

—

Chronology
Background and References

Chronology : Germany June 1932 – July 1933

1932

1 June The Catholic Centre Party's Heinrich Brüning, having presided over a catastrophic economic collapse, loses the support of the Reichspresident and is replaced as Chancellor by the arch conservative Franz von Papen.

3 June Parliament (der Reichstag) is dissolved and a new election set for 31 July. The election campaign is marked by violent clashes between opposing paramilitaries.

31 July The Nazi Party wins 230 seats in the Reichstag, replacing the Social Democrats as the largest party in parliament but falling short of an absolute majority.

13 August Adolf Hitler demands the chancellorship for himself but is rebuffed by Reichspresident Paul von Hindenburg.

17–19 August The Catholic bishops reiterate their prohibition on Catholics joining the Nazi Party, first issued following the Reichstag election of September 1930, but allow priests discretion in applying the ban.

August–September Centre Party leaders negotiate with the Nazi Party over a possible coalition government, but no agreement is reached.

12 September The Reichstag is dissolved. A new Reichstag election is announced for 6 November.

6 November Nazi Party representation in the Reichstag falls to 196 seats, but the Nazis remain the largest party in parliament.

3 December Kurt von Schleicher, former army officer and confidant of the Reichspresident, replaces Franz von Papen as Chancellor. von Schleicher proposes to form a cabinet which includes social democratic trade unionists and 'left-wing' Nazis who favour publicly financed employment-creation schemes. Social Democrat and Nazi leaders quash these plans.

1933

January The Reichspresident, unhappy with von Schleicher's willingness to countenance 'socialist' economic policies, tacitly supports secret negotiations between von Papen and Hitler to form a new cabinet.

28 January von Schleicher and his cabinet resign.

30 January Adolf Hitler is appointed Chancellor by the Reichspresident. The new cabinet contains two Nazis in addition to Hitler, along with some traditional conservatives. Franz von Papen is Deputy Chancellor.

1 February The Reichstag is dissolved and new elections are announced for 5 March. The election campaign is again marked by violent clashes between rival paramilitaries.

17 February An election statement from leading Catholic lay organisations sharply criticises political extremism and warns of the dangers of dictatorship.

20 February The Catholic Bishops' Conference issues an election statement exhorting Catholics to vote for candidates who have shown themselves to be true friends of peace, the Christian religion and the Catholic Church.

27 February The Reichstag building is set on fire and severely damaged.

28 February The government declares a state of emergency and passes a new law allowing the detention of suspects without charge. Several anti-Nazi newspapers are banned and Nazi militia attacks increase.

5 March The Nazi Party wins 288 seats in the Reichstag election, sufficient with the support of a smaller traditional right-wing party to form an absolute majority.

21 March The Nazis use the ceremony in Potsdam marking the opening of the new Reichstag to create the impression of continuity between the new regime and the conservative, nationalistic traditions of Germany.

23 March The Enabling Act, which formally empowers Adolf Hitler to rule without recourse to parliament for the following four years, passes the Reichstag. After much internal debate the two Catholic parties, the Centre Party and the Bavarian Peoples' Party, support the Act. The Social Democrats vote against it. Communist MPs have either been arrested or are in hiding.

29–30 March The German Catholic bishops publish a statement withdrawing their long-standing prohibitions and warnings in respect of the Nazis.

1 April The persecution of Jews in Germany begins with a government sanctioned call to boycott Jewish professionals and businesses.

20 July A concordat specifying the rights of the Catholic Church in the Third Reich is formally signed by representatives of the Holy See and the German government. The concordat is ratified on 10 September 1933.

Background and References

Background

The Vanguard is modelled on the 'Sturmschar' (storm troop), a self-styled elite group formed in 1929 from elements of various German Catholic young men's organisations. In depicting the Vanguard I drew on Börger & Schroer and Götz von Olenhusen.

The two papal encyclicals referred to in the story are *Rerum Novarum, On Capital and Labour*, Pope Leo XIII, 15 May 1891, and *Quadragesimo Anno, On Reconstruction of the Social Order*, Pope Pius XI, 15 May 1931. English versions are available at *http://www.papalencyclicals.net/document-directory*. This website and the websites cited below were last accessed on 31 December 2018.

The song excerpts that appear in 'Saturday 29 – Sunday 30 October 1932' come from *Wir sind jung, die Welt is offen* and *Bundeslied*. The two songs are taken from the collection *Das Singeschiff*.

'Brother, Can You Spare a Dime?', the song Bobby O'Donnell reacts to in 'Thursday 24 November 1932', was written in 1930 by lyricist E. Y. 'Yip' Harburg and composer Jay Gorney.

The Catholic newspaper that Frank reads in Father Schapp's presbytery on the Day of Potsdam is modelled on *Der Gerade Weg* (*The Straight Path*). The paper's editor, Fritz Gerlich, was imprisoned shortly after the 5 March 1933 election and kept in detention until his murder by the Nazis during the so-called Night of the Long Knives on 30 June 1934. *Der Gerade Weg* is available at *https://www.bayerische-landesbibliothek-online.de/der-gerade-weg*.

A recording of the speeches given by Paul von Hindenburg and Adolf Hitler on the Day of Potsdam is available at *https://www.youtube.com/watch?v=AzCGAeOvPyU*. The text of Hitler's speech can be found at *https://www.1000dokumente.de/pdf/dok_0005_tag_de.pdf*.

The English translation of the sentence from the German Catholic bishops' statement withdrawing their prohibitions against the Nazis, quoted in 'Wednesday 29 March 1933', comes from Scholder, p.252.

In the carnival scenes I drew on Haffner. In presenting Stormy Weather's views on belief I drew on Cohen.

Original German versions of the Church documents referred to in the story can be found in Müller and Stasiewski.

References

Börger, Bernd & Hans Schroer (eds) *Sie hielten stand: Sturmschar im Katholischen Jungmännerverband Deutschlands*, Verlag Haus Altenberg, Düsseldorf, 1989.

Cohen, L. Jonathan, *An Essay on Belief and Acceptance*, Oxford University Press, New York, 1992.

Cornwell, John, *Hitler's Pope: The Secret History of Pius X11*, Penguin, London, 2000.

Götz von Olenhusen, Irmtraud, *Jugendreich, Gottesreich, Deutsches Reich: Junge Generation, Religion und Politik 1928–1933*, Verlag Wissenschaft und Politik, Köln, 1987.

Haffner, Sebastian, *Defying Hitler: A Memoir*, trans. Oliver Pretzel, Weidenfeld & Nicolson, London, 2002.

Katholischer Jungmännerverband Deutschlands, *Das Singeschiff: Lieder deutscher katholischer Jugend*, Jugendhaus Düsseldorf, 1930.

Müller, Hans, *Katholische Kirche und Nationalsozialismus, Dokumente 1930–1935*, Nymphenburger Verlagshandlung, München, 1962.

Scholder, Klaus, *The Churches and the Third Reich, Vol. 1, Preliminary History and the Time of Illusions 1918–1934*, trans. John Bowden, SCM Press, London, 1987.

Stasiewski, Bernhard, *Akten Deutscher Bischöfe über die Lage der Kirche 1933-1945, Band 1, 1933–1934*, Kommission für Zeitgeschichte, Mainz 1968.